The
$150,000
Rugelach

The $150,000 Rugelach

Allison & Wayne Marks

YELLOW
JACKET

This is a work of fiction. Any references to historical events, real people, or real places are used fictitiously. Other names, characters, places, and events are products of the author's imagination, and any resemblance to actual events or places or persons, living or dead, is entirely coincidental.

 YELLOW JACKET
an imprint of Little Bee Books

New York, NY
Text copyright © 2021 by Allison Marks and Wayne Marks
All rights reserved, including the right of reproduction
in whole or in part in any form.
Yellow Jacket and associated colophon are
trademarks of Little Bee Books.
Interior designed by Natalie Padberg Bartoo
For information about special discounts on bulk purchases,
please contact Little Bee Books at sales@littlebeebooks.com.
Manufactured in China RRD 0521
First Edition
10 9 8 7 6 5 4 3 2 1
Library of Congress Cataloging-in-Publication
Data is available upon request.
ISBN 978-1-4998-1210-7 (hardcover)
ISBN 978-1-4998-1211-4 (ebook)
yellowjacketreads.com

To Rita Marks

thank you for all the sweet memories

Chapter 1

Jillian Mermelstein stared at the long wooden spoon lying next to the empty mixing bowl. It had been months since she had thought about this scarred brown utensil, usually hidden in the kitchen junk drawer underneath a pizza take-out menu. She ran her index finger over its curved top, where a small triangle of wood was missing like a chipped tooth.

She closed her eyes and gripped the handle hard, hoping it would magically make her feel joyful and inspired, like it once did. Instead, the spoon felt cold and dead—a stick of tiger maple with a chunk missing, a reminder that her life would always be slightly broken, forever incomplete.

Jillian placed the old spoon back in the drawer. She wouldn't need it today.

Clutching a flathead screwdriver and a bundle of wires, Grandma Rita strolled into the room as Jillian closed the drawer. "I've been working on that busted garage door opener all morning," she said, unbuckling her tool belt and placing it on a chair. "Seems to be a faulty sensor. Oooh, is that a mixing bowl I see? Is somebody thinking about doing some baking?"

To anyone who knew her, Grandma Rita was the most loving person on the planet. Her bright smile and kind eyes could light a million candles. Sometimes she wore pink highlights in her graying hair "just because." She was the best kind of crazy.

Grandma Rita picked a flier off the refrigerator. "Say, you still have to take something to your sixth-grade winter party, right? It says here, *bring cookies, brownies, or other baked goods*. What'll it be?"

Suddenly the only thing Jillian wanted was to run to her room and escape within the pages of the thickest book she could find. Reading was how she spent most of her evenings and all of her weekends. It was the perfect way to avoid conversations like this one.

No reason to change my routine tonight, especially for a stupid class party.

"Come on, Jilly. It'll be fun," Grandma Rita said, doing her best to sound cheerful for her granddaughter's sake. "Let's fill the house with the smell of fresh almond cookies."

Jillian crossed her arms. Her jet-black ponytail swayed as she shook her head. She gazed down at her tennis shoes, unwilling to look her grandmother in the eye. Her skin was unusually pale, not like last year when her summer tan lasted all through the winter. She just didn't feel much like going outside anymore, not even to hike on wooded trails or pick wild blackberries.

"No. I don't want to."

Grandma Rita persisted. "How about we make chocolate rugelach instead? I bet your friends at school would love that."

Jillian frowned. Since moving with her father to Ardmore, Ohio, from Seattle in September, she hadn't made any friends at Sieberling School. She didn't want any. And she certainly didn't want to spend an afternoon making chocolate rugelach, or almond cookies, or anything for *anyone*. Watching her classmates wolf down their lunches, never pausing to actually taste the food, made her doubt that they would appreciate her rugelach—a traditional Jewish pastry filled with a spiral of chocolate tucked between layers of flaky dough.

"I can't. Too much homework."

"Then I'll just have to make the rugelach myself." Grandma Rita went to the cupboard and began gathering ingredients, none of which had any business being in a rugelach recipe.

Argh! Soy sauce? Not soy sauce, Grandma!

Jillian laughed to herself. As a part-time math professor, Grandma Rita had an amazing way of simplifying the story problems in Jillian's homework. She could replace a leaky faucet, install an electrical socket, change the oil in her roadster, and run the annual Ardmore Thanksgiving Day 10K in under an hour and five minutes.

But no matter how much Grandma Rita tried, baking was not part of her skill set. Her pound cake weighed a ton. Her sugar cookies were too salty and her salted caramel cupcakes were too sweet. Once, smoke from a blueberry pie left in the oven too long brought a prompt visit from the Ardmore Fire Department. Jillian feared that her grandmother's solo attempt at rugelach might have even worse results.

"Yes, siree, gonna make the world's best chocolate rugelach for Jilly's class," Grandma Rita said, whistling as she picked up a cheese grater and glanced at Jillian out of the corner of her eye. "Sorry you don't want to help, but, hey, I'll do just fine . . . all . . . by . . . myself."

Jillian thought about the wooden spoon, which used to feel so warm. So comforting. It had belonged to her mother—Grandma Rita's daughter, Joan. Mom had taught Jillian how to bake in the kitchen of Joan of Hearts, the pastry shop she had owned in Seattle. Her mother had shown her the secrets of making rugelach: letting the butter soften, not overmixing the ingredients, properly chilling the dough, turning each bite-size morsel golden brown, and knowing the precise instant to pull it from the oven.

Now her mother was gone.

Jillian picked up the spoon and recalled her mother's words at the end of her first baking lesson.

Don't forget to add the most important ingredient of all. Love. Trust me, without it, your rugelach won't taste nearly as sweet. Nothing will.

"Fine, Grandma, I'll help you," Jillian sighed.

"Wonderful! I'll put on Vivaldi. Your mother always listened to classical music when she baked."

"Yes, I remember."

"So, my dearest pâtissier, where do we begin?"

"First, put away the cheese grater and soy sauce. We won't need them."

"Of course, I knew that," Grandma Rita said, winking.

Chapter 2

Across town, Jack Fineman spun around the kitchen to the sound of his favorite rock band, Zombie Brunch. Holding a bottle of vanilla extract in one hand and a whisk in the other, he thrashed his head in sync to the screaming guitars and industrial noises. He tossed his mad-scientist tangle of hair from side to side and shouted out the song's first verse:

Yeah, yeah, yeah, yeah, yeah, yeah, yeah!
Maniacs, it's time to munch!
Yeah, yeah, yeah, yeah, yeah, yeah, yeah!
Welcome to the Zombie Bruuuuunch!

The granite countertop was all but hidden under ingredients and gadgets Jack needed to create "my next masterpiece," as he called it. Tomorrow at the sixth-grade class party, he knew everyone would be anticipating his latest delectable dessert. He didn't want to disappoint his fans.

"So what are you making this year?" his best friend, Chad, had asked at lunch. "It's going to be hard to top those little pies with the weird green fruit on top you made last year."

"Oh, you mean my kiwi-crowned tartlets with strawberry filling and rosemary-tinged pretzel crust," Jack had said. "I have something even better planned, but you'll have to wait. World-famous chefs never reveal their secrets."

"World famous? Get real."

"Gotta dream big. Gotta dream big."

For Chad and the rest of the class at Sieberling School, the day of the holiday party was no big deal: sugary treats, carbonated punch, a crossword puzzle, crafts, and a song or two.

But to Jack, the holiday party meant more. It was his Super Bowl, his World Cup, and his victory lap at the Daytona Speedway rolled into one.

That's because Jack Fineman had one goal—to be the greatest pastry chef who ever lived. Not second best or only good enough to win praise from Chad or Amy Eppington, the girl he'd had a crush on since first grade. He wanted to be *the* best. Nothing else would do. And in Jack's mind, nothing else mattered.

According to Jack's plan, foodies from Ohio to France would one day savor his éclairs and cream puffs. His face would appear on his own brand of spices and cookware—stainless steel spatulas, nesting bowls, Dutch ovens, and more. Lines of customers stretching blocks would snake outside his gourmet pastry shops. He would be recognized as the most famous person ever to come from Ardmore.

But right now the title of Ardmore's most famous culinary resident belonged to Jack's idol, Phineas Farnsworth III, owner and CEO of the world-renowned Farnsworth Baking Supply Company. The Farnsworth baking dynasty began in the 1930s as nothing more than a humble one-room store run by Phineas Farnsworth III's grandfather. Now the factory in the center of the city took up three entire blocks. Practically half the town worked for the business, churning out mountains of flour, rivers of lemon extract, blizzards of powdered sugar, and kitchen gadgets of every kind. Because of the Farnsworth family, Ardmore was known everywhere as "Bakerstown, USA." For the last seventy-four years, the company had sponsored the Bakerstown Bonanza, a contest that drew amateur pastry chefs from across the country to Ardmore. In the world of cupcakes and cookies, Jack knew there was no one bigger than Phineas Farnsworth III.

Jack looked down at a package of brown sugar featuring a cartoonish drawing of Farnsworth in a white chef's hat, winking and giving a thumbs-up.

Someday that'll be me, Jack thought, as he cracked his knuckles and scanned his original recipe for butterscotch basil brownies.

"Let the *Jack Attack* begin!" he roared.

Jack put on his own chef's hat and slipped on a blue apron over his ripped T-shirt and shredded jeans. Like a medieval sorcerer brewing a bubbling potion, he tossed ingredients into the mixing bowl: butter, brown sugar, salt, eggs, flour, baking soda, vanilla extract, butterscotch chips, and chopped basil leaves. Jack barely looked at the recipe. His fingers knew how much to add and when to hold back. Flour dusted his hair. Batter splattered his apron.

With the mixer whirring, Jack belted out lyrics to the second cut on Zombie Brunch's only album, *Enjoy the Feast.* Released in 1977, it had been panned by critics as "the worst music ever put on vinyl." Jack loved it.

> *Yeah, yeah, yeah, yeah, yeah, yeah, yeah!*
> *The moon is down, now comes the sun!*
> *Yeah, yeah, yeah, yeah, yeah, yeah, yeah!*
> *Put down your fork! The meal is done!*

"Jack, please!" Mr. Fineman said, poking his head into the kitchen. "I'm reviewing some new tax laws. I need to concentrate. Can you sing inside your head or something?"

Mrs. Fineman followed. "I just got off the phone with a patient. She asked me if everything was okay at our house because it sounded like someone was in pain."

"Sorry," Jack said. "I'll dial it down."

"Good. Now finish up and do your homework," Mr. Fineman said before going back to his stack of papers.

Jack breathed a sigh of relief. He had expected another long talk about spending too many hours with his head in a cookbook and not enough time studying the Mesopotamians or the structure of a water molecule. He recalled his last report card (one B, three C's, and a D in social studies). This had earned him an extended lecture about the importance of schoolwork and a three-week ban from the kitchen. At least this time his father's message was short and to the point.

But it wasn't just his grades. From early on, Jack sensed something annoyed his parents about his baking. He just couldn't figure out what it was.

Refocusing on his masterpiece, Jack poured the batter into the greased pan and slid it into the oven. As he was cleaning up, he imagined himself as a contestant in the Bakerstown Bonanza. Cell phones held up by the crowd captured his every move for posterity. He envisioned Farnsworth watching open-mouthed, unable to grasp how someone so young could be so talented in the kitchen.

The ding of the oven timer brought Jack back to reality. He iced the brownies with cinnamon cream and breathed in deeply. By the aroma alone, Jack knew they would be the talk of Sieberling School for another year. A creation so spectacular that even the great chefs of Europe would turn in their aprons after a single taste. He smiled, certain that by tomorrow afternoon he would take the next step up the ladder to culinary greatness.

Chapter 3

Jack laid his circular tray of butterscotch basil brownies in the middle of the long table by the blackboard. He had cut them into small pieces to form a Star of David. Wooden dreidels and white chocolate balls wrapped in blue foil decorated the plate. He stepped back, pleased that he had added a touch of his Jewish heritage to the table.

Magnificent! You've outdone yourself, Mr. Fineman. Once again, Jack pictured Farnsworth complimenting him while twirling his long braided goatee.

Jack reviewed the rest of the holiday goodies placed beneath paper snowflakes hanging from the ceiling. He saw store-bought sugar cookies topped with waxy green icing, lumpy chocolate cupcakes with a white gumdrop protruding from the top, jelly donuts oozing raspberry filling, caramel-coated popcorn balls dotted with unexploded kernels, a tin of peppermint candy canes, some dry snickerdoodles, and potato chips with French onion dip. In the center, a clear plastic punch bowl held a fizzing blend of ginger ale and neon lime fruit drink the color of antifreeze.

Jack turned to go back to his desk when he spied something peculiar nestled between a lopsided Styrofoam snowman and a pyramid of red plastic cups. His nose led him past the donuts and cupcakes to a white plate filled with . . .

Chocolate rugelach? Who made chocolate rugelach?

Jack glanced at Chad, who was staring at the snow outside. He assumed his friend was daydreaming about snowboarding or filming a new video to add to his YouTube channel of skateboarding tricks—many of which involved him accidentally colliding with a road sign.

Nope, it's definitely not Chad. He thinks a Twinkie and a root beer is a gourmet meal.

Jack bent closer to the plate. He hated to admit it, but the rugelach smelled wonderful.

Not to worry. It probably tastes like wet cardboard filled with cheap chocolate. Guaranteed.

"Okay, class. Take your seats," said Ms. Riedel, the homeroom teacher. "Before we start the party, we're going to do a story problem."

The class groaned.

"Math?" Chad muttered to Jack. "What kind of warped holiday celebration is this? Ho, ho, ho! What would you

13

like for Christmas, little Timmy? Of course, an algebra equation!"

Chad's banter usually made Jack crack up . . . and get in trouble. But not this time. Jack was too busy scanning the room to find the secret rugelach-maker—the person with the chutzpah to challenge the Sieberling School top baker throne, which he had held since wowing his first-grade class with milk chocolate–burgundy cherry cookies.

"I have a special surprise for the student who figures out the problem first," Ms. Riedel continued.

Her words grabbed Jack's attention. Ms. Riedel was known for stashing the best rewards in her bottom desk drawer. And this was no exception. She held up a dark chocolate bar flavored with spiced orange peels, one of Jack's favorite flavor combinations. He believed no one in the class could appreciate the blend of cocoa and citrus like him.

That bar belongs to me.

Ms. Riedel wrote the problem on the board:

At the holiday party in Room 609, the table was filled with 100 treats: 25 candy canes, 20 chocolate cupcakes, 20 brownies, 7 popcorn balls, 1 bag of chips, 1 container of French onion dip, and 1 bowl of punch. The rest are jelly donuts. What percentage of the holiday treats are jelly donuts?

"Now . . . go! Show your work. And no guessing. Raise your hand when you think you've got it."

The class feverishly scribbled in their notebooks. Jack was usually a whiz at math, especially percentages. But the lingering smell of the rugelach distracted him.

Chad, not much for quizzes, or math, or homework, doodled a blizzard scene in the margins of his paper.

"Don't look at me for the answer," Chad said. "I'm busy freestyling down the Matterhorn right now."

Jack stared at the board. Then his brain clicked. *That's it. Add the numbers and subtract the total from one hundred. Boom, there's the answer.*

Jack's hand shot up. Ms. Riedel looked past him to the last row, the desk on the very end next to the storage closet.

"Yes, Jillian. So what did you come up with?"

"Twenty-five percent," Jillian said in a barely audible voice. "One-fourth of the holiday treats are jelly donuts."

"Excellent work!" Ms. Riedel said with a hint of surprise in her voice, handing her the chocolate bar.

It was the first time Jillian had raised her hand all year and one of the few occasions when she had spoken in class.

Jack had never said a word to Jillian, nor had she ever said as much as hi to him. Chad thought her name was Nancy.

"And now that you've all worked up a good appetite, it's time to eat," Ms. Riedel said.

Let the fun begin, Jack thought.

Students sprung from their seats. Like a swarm of locusts descending on a Kansas wheat field, they devoured Jack's brownies until only half a piece and a streak of cinnamon icing remained. Jillian went last, filling a cup with punch and taking the last brownie, which she ate at her desk.

Success! Jack thought, a satisfied grin covering his face as he pictured himself cutting the ribbon during the opening of his first pastry shop.

"Dude, those were incredible," Chad said, picking at the crumbs on his T-shirt.

Jeremy Crawford, the class president, gave Jack a high five. Frieda Johnston returned to the table and moaned, "The brownies are gone!" Ms. Riedel asked for the recipe. But amongst the praise, Jack heard more than a few mentions of a dessert other than his own.

"Did you try that strange chocolate thingy? One word . . . wow!"

"That was soooo good!"

"Best . . . cookie . . . ever! Best . . . treat . . . ever!" Amy Eppington said. Jack suspected she wasn't talking about the sugar cookies purchased at the local Food Mart.

It drove him insane.

Crush canceled!

When the final bell rang, Jack casually approached the

plate of rugelach. Only Ms. Riedel and Jillian were left in the room.

This was *not* a hard story problem for Jack to solve. He knew in an instant the rugelach belonged to the quiet girl with the desk near the storage closet. Yes, the rugelach smelled fantastic, but the true test was how it tasted.

Jack picked up the final piece, a small lopsided crescent, the outcast of the batch, sitting like a quiet classmate who just wants to be left alone. He popped it into his mouth and chewed, quickly at first, then slowly, as the blend of chocolate and cream cheese tingled his taste buds.

Jillian looked up just as a frown formed on Jack's face. A look of disgust followed, like he had been served rotten cabbage. She jerked her head back down.

Jack collected his plate and left without saying a word.

He had never tasted anything so delicious. Never.

Chapter 4

Back home, Jillian placed the chocolate-streaked plate in the sink next to the wooden spoon, still spackled with batter from last night.

"So how was the party?" Grandma Rita asked. "I bet our rugelach was a big hit!"

Jillian ignored her grandmother and went straight to her room, tiptoeing by her father who was asleep on the couch. Mr. Mermelstein worked two jobs to support them, one during the day and the other at night. Jillian rarely got the chance to spend time with him except for Sunday mornings when they played Scrabble. This was mostly how Jillian saw him—exhausted and snoring like a low-flying jet.

She lay on her bed and replayed the events of her day. First, the positives: She had answered the math problem and received a chocolate bar. She had heard some of her classmates talk about her rugelach like it was a gift beamed down from heaven. For a brief moment, she had felt . . . happy.

But when Jillian closed her eyes, none of those things mattered. All she saw was the twisted expression on Jack's long, thin face. She hugged the raccoon hand puppet her mother had given her on her third birthday. Like the wooden spoon, it only recently had come out of storage.

He's the boy who made the butterscotch basil brownies shaped like a Star of David, she thought. *He would know what rugelach should taste like. And he absolutely hated it.*

In that instant, Jillian missed her mother stroking her long black hair and telling her that everything would be okay. As she started to remember, a tidal wave of memories washed over her. Some were of the happiest moments of her life. Trips to Silver Creek Lake, where she, her mother, and her father built sand fortresses and ate rainbow-colored snow cones until the sun sank low. The three of them riding bicycles through cool pine forests on a fall morning. The sound of giggles as they ate pretzel sticks during games of gin rummy and Uno.

These memories always gave Jillian the strength to move forward. On her best days, she knew in her heart that there would be good times again. There would be light. And she hoped that someday there would even be laughter. But it hadn't been easy to think that way today.

I made the rugelach just how you showed me. What went wrong?

Jillian thought back to her first baking lesson soon after her seventh birthday. She loved being in the kitchen of her mother's new pastry shop, especially at five o'clock on a Saturday morning, long before customers trickled in. It was just the two of them, shelves full of ingredients, and endless possibilities. After her mother had completed the day's pastries, she looked at Jillian.

"So, Jilly, what should we make together on this fine Seattle morning?"

"We?"

"Yes, we."

"Rugelach! Chocolate rugelach! Pleeaaaase!"

"A superb suggestion, my dear."

Under her mother's direction, Jillian spooned cream cheese and butter into a ceramic mixing bowl to make the dough. Next, they added sugar, salt, vanilla extract, and finally the flour. Together, they held the tiger maple spoon and blended the ingredients until they were smooth.

"Now the chocolate, right? Lots of it!" Jillian pleaded. "It's what makes your rugelach the best—better than what I ate at the deli and ten times yummier than what you get at the grocery store."

"Ah, Jilly, cooking is not a contest," her mother said, cupping her daughter's chin with floured fingers. "It is a prayer whispered humbly as the sun rises. When no one else is looking. When the rest of the world sleeps."

"Yes, but hurry. I'm getting hungry!"

"Patience, Jilly. There will always be time for chocolate. Lots of it. Today, tomorrow, for as long as you're my girl."

Jillian dried her tears with her sleeve. Her mother had been wrong. There wouldn't be more time. Shortly after Jillian's tenth birthday, her mother became ill. She recalled those days in a blur of snapshots: her parents talking behind closed doors, months of treatments, rows of pill bottles, a white-coated worker setting up a hospital bed in the living room, a late-night visit from the rabbi, Grandma Rita's swollen eyes hidden behind dark sunglasses during the funeral.

Jillian forced herself to remember more. Returning home from the cemetery, she had walked into the kitchen. It felt ghostly. She saw her mother opening cupboards. Kneading dough for a challah. Reciting the Sabbath prayers. She smelled a hint of jasmine flowers, which her mother wore in her hair, and heard Vivaldi's *The Four Seasons* playing. It was the section called "Spring," her mother's favorite season. A time of renewal . . . of hope . . .

In the weeks that followed, those images faded, replaced by the harsh reality of more family troubles. Jillian learned the pastry shop had left them in severe debt. Her mother's dream of owning a little place to bake and sell her cookies, pies, tarts, and tortes from family recipes was a gamble, especially in Seattle, a city with coffee shops and cafés on every corner. But her parents had done it, anyway.

"Oh, honey, if you don't have a dream to keep you going,

you're just sleepwalking through life," her mother had told Jillian the day Joan of Hearts Pastry Shop opened.

Friends and patrons packed the store on its first day. A fiddler and mandolinist played bluegrass in the corner as streams of people flowed in and out. A local food reporter came to interview Jillian's mother. Afterward, she proudly displayed the framed article next to the cash register. The headline read, *Joan Mermelstein Brings Baked Heaven to the Heart of Seattle.*

"Someday this shop will be yours, Jillian," her mother had said. "We're off to a great start."

Despite her mother's hard work and the shop's loyal customers, bills mounted. Her father lost his job at an advertising firm while caring for her mother. They owed the bank thousands of dollars. Soon after her death, hard decisions had to be made.

"We have to sell all the pastry shop equipment—the mixers, ovens, coolers," her father had said. "Even then, we won't have enough money to stay here. Grandma Rita said we could move in with her in Ohio until we can get back on our feet. I'm so sorry."

At Sieberling School, Jillian decided to keep to herself. She did not want to share her past with strangers. And in her new city, everyone was a stranger.

"Let's give a warm welcome to your new classmate, Jillian Mermelstein," Ms. Riedel had said on her first day.

Jillian walked directly to the back row, looking down to avoid the pairs of eyes watching her.

Jillian was pulled back from her memories when Grandma Rita gently knocked on the door.

"Do you want to talk?"

"Not really."

Grandma Rita came in anyway. Sitting on the edge of the bed she asked, "So?"

"So what?"

"So, did your friends eat all the rugelach?"

"Grandma, I don't have any friends here. And, yes, everyone loved it except for this one boy."

"There's always one in every bunch, isn't there? I bet he wouldn't know a good rugelach if it knocked him on the head. So your day wasn't all bad?"

Jillian pulled the chocolate bar out of her backpack.

"No, not all bad. I won this."

"How?"

"By solving a math problem about percentages."

"That's my girl." Grandma Rita took the bar and broke it in half. "What do you say? Fifty percent for you and fifty percent for me?"

"Deal," Jillian said, taking a bite and letting the sweetness roll around her tongue.

Chapter 5

Jack paced in the kitchen, chugging a glass of milk to wash away the taste of Jillian's chocolate rugelach. It would haunt him for days.

My butterscotch basil brownies were epic. I tested the recipe. My presentation was perfect. The results spectacular. But the rugelach was better. A hundred times better.

The more Jack sulked around the kitchen, the worse he felt—his Foodie Olympics ruined. He wasn't just troubled by the rugelach. It seemed as if someone had thrown a rusty spatula into the well-oiled gears of his lifelong plans.

How am I going to be the world's greatest pastry chef if I'm not even the best in Ms. Riedel's sixth-grade class?

Jack knew his rugelach. He had gorged on different flavors at family parties: pumpkin spice, cherry, blueberry, apricot, coconut, and banana. What he had sampled earlier that day, though, made all other attempts taste like carpet glue.

In need of an ego boost, he texted Chad:

> Great holiday party!

Other than the math, yeah.

> You liked the brownies?

I told you, man, they were great. Your best ever! Even better than your little pies.

> Tartlets. Did you try any of the other desserts?

A weird chocolate cookie.

> Oh, yeah! It's called rugelach. What did you think?

Chad didn't reply. Jack felt his frustration rising again.

> Hello? What did you think of the rugelach?

It was okay. Who brought it?

The girl in the back row.

Nancy?

No, her name is Jillian.

Jack put down his phone when a thought crossed his mind.

Wait a minute! Jillian brought *them to school, but did she bake them? What if her mother made them for her? Or she bought them at that gourmet pastry shop in Wooster? There's no evidence that she made them! Boom, that's the answer! I'm still the king!*

Jack felt better until his brother entered the kitchen. Tall with muscular arms, Bruce wore mauve and aquamarine checkered slacks, a fuchsia polo shirt, and an orange visor. A golf bag crammed with clubs capped with knitted covers hung over his shoulder. As a member of the high school golf team, Bruce obsessed about how to hit the middle of the fairway on a windy day, or what grip to use when striking a ball off the lip of a sand trap. During the winter he practiced for hours at the indoor driving range next to Speedy Wash.

Golf was one of Bruce's two passions. The other was making Jack's life miserable.

"Hey, it's Baron Von Bundt Cake home from school," Bruce said, messing up Jack's hair.

Jack had grown used to Bruce's corny nicknames. The

Pillsbury Dough Dork ranked at the bottom along with Betty Crocked and Batter for Brains.

"By the way, the kitchen reeked last night," Bruce continued. "What sewage were you throwing together for that holiday party? Haven't you learned yet that this baking thing of yours is a waste of time?"

Jack stopped himself from blurting out, *And chasing a little white ball around a cow pasture isn't?* He knew better than to confront his brother. After all, Bruce was taller, stronger, and had clubs handy.

Bruce opened the refrigerator door and took out the same thing he ate every day after school: two slices of bologna on white bread slathered with mayonnaise. Jack shook his head. He wondered what kind of cosmic joke paired him with an older brother who had such picky eating habits and bad taste in clothing.

Their parents still told the story of Bruce's early eating experiences. Years ago as a baby, he spit out his first spoonful of creamed spinach. He scrunched up his face and yowled, looking nothing like the cherub-faced infant on the baby food jar. Mashed peas produced even more volcanic results. He spewed the vegetable onto the white wall in front of him, forming a piece of modern art referred to by his parents as a work from Bruce's "green period."

Even at sixteen, Bruce threw fits if the creamed corn on his plate made the slightest contact with his baked beans, or if a tuna casserole dared to ooze into the domain of a buttered roll.

"No touching! Foods must not touch!" Bruce always insisted.

So when Mrs. Fineman played "here comes the choo-choo" and gave Jack his first taste of solid food—a dollop of strained beets—she covered her ears and prepared for a similar eruption.

Instead, Jack closed his eyes in ecstasy as his taste buds danced the hora. A smile spread across his face.

At that moment, six-month-old Jack said his first word: "Yum!" He opened his mouth so wide that a steam locomotive pulling several beet-filled boxcars could have easily rocketed past his toothless gums.

This first spoonful of root vegetable marked the beginning of Jack's love of food. He gobbled up everything: mangos, okra, cabbage, papayas, kale, yams, cucumbers, artichoke hearts, and Swiss chard.

This annoyed Bruce to no end.

"If Jack can eat it, so can you," their parents said.

"He doesn't know any better," Bruce argued. "He'll grow out of it."

But Jack didn't.

Instead of gulping down a bite, Jack rolled it around in his mouth, judging its texture and flavor before sending it southward to his stomach.

When Jack was nine months old, his parents noticed

he seemed to have developed a rating system for the meals they prepared:

Whoop of Joy: ★★★★★
Wide Grin: ★★★★
Shrug: ★★★
Big Frown: ★★
Food Splattered on Floor: ★

On his first birthday, Jack received a small Boston cream pie of his very own. He grasped a mixture of chocolate icing, vanilla custard, and moist cake in his right hand. Sniffing the mushy mess, he shoved it into his mouth, smearing most of it across his face.

That's when Jack added two words to his expanding vocabulary: "MORE! NOW!"

Handful after handful disappeared until not a speck remained. Jack howled with delight.

"I guess that would rate a ten," Mrs. Fineman said, pulling the plate out of Jack's clutches.

Jack banged his fists on the table. "MORE! NOW!" he repeated.

By the age of three, Jack was using his Little Chef Baker's Oven, heated by a single light bulb, to make multilayered iced tarts for his parents.

"Did you try this?" Mr. Fineman asked. "It is *really* good!"

"I know," Mrs. Fineman replied. "No doubt about it, he has genuine baking talent, like my grandmother, Bubbe Leah. But . . ."

"You're worried he'll end up like her, right?" Mr. Fineman said.

"Yes. I don't want that to happen."

"We'll have to see how it all plays out. For now, just take another bite and enjoy."

"Mmm . . . definitely five stars!"

Once Bruce had finished his bologna sandwich, he turned his attention back to Jack.

"You didn't answer me. What was that sickening smell in the kitchen last night?"

"My own recipe for butterscotch basil brownies."

"It can never be just chocolate or vanilla with you. Why do you always mess it up with something weird, like basil?"

"There is more to life than chocolate and vanilla."

"You're right. There's strawberry, too!"

"I give up."

Chapter 6

Jillian waited at the kitchen table for her father to return home from the late shift at the auto parts warehouse. Since moving to Ardmore, he spent his nights packing exhaust pipes and pistons in boxes to be shipped to mechanics around the world. During the afternoons, he hunched over legal documents in an office cubicle checking for poor grammar and misspellings.

Before her sat a Scrabble board, two wooden racks, a velvet bag filled with letter tiles, a scorecard, and a pencil. Every five minutes, she watched for the headlights of her father's Chevy Cavalier pulling into the driveway. She looked forward all week to this Sunday morning ritual—a game of Scrabble on his only day off.

Jillian squeezed her father's thin frame when he arrived,

lunch pail tucked under his arm. His dark eyebrows were lightly frosted with snow and his tired eyes begged for some needed rest.

"How's my little wordsmith today?" he asked, kissing her forehead.

"Fine. I'm feeling lucky this morning."

"Jills, Scrabble isn't about luck. It's about making the best out of the letters you're given."

Jillian knew this was partially true. If you studied hard, you could make a major score out of what looked like an impossible mishmash of tiles. From *The Official Scrabble Players Dictionary*, she memorized all the Q words that didn't need a U, such as qadi, qiblas, and qindarka. She wrote out lists of odd three-letter words like nim, rya, and yag, and jotted down eight-letter words from aardvark to zymogene that would be worth fifty bonus points when all tiles were played at once. And she could recite all the acceptable Scrabble two-letter words, including ef, gi, pe, xi, and her favorite, oy, which her father said a lot lately.

Still, her father remained undefeated. When the game was close, the letter she needed hid deep within the bag. In her mind, that was the very definition of luck. Bad luck.

They each pulled a tile out of the bag to determine who would go first. Jillian grabbed an E and her father a T.

"You're up, Jills. The letter closest to A goes first.

Take it easy on your poor dad. It's been a long night."

Jillian took seven tiles and placed them on her rack. *CRCZJII.* She shuffled the tiles in every possible way. Cici was a proper name—not acceptable. So was Ric. She wished there was a blank tile for Z, an A, and a U to spell jacuzzi, or a T to spell critic. Rizi looked like it might be a word but wasn't. Five minutes passed.

"I can't make a word," she said.

"Not a single one?

"No."

"That's almost impossible on a first rack. A million-to-one occurrence."

"No, just my bad luck," she said.

Mr. Mermelstein looked down at his own rack: *GHPQOAE.*

He arranged the letters to read *HOPE* and turned the rack around for Jillian.

"Well how about that? One of your mother's favorite words," he said.

Jillian smiled slightly before gazing at her rack of letters and shaking her head in frustration.

"Is there anything you'd like to talk about?" her father asked. "I know I'm not around as much as I'd like to be right now. I'm used to hard work, but two jobs is a bit much, even for me."

"I've been thinking a lot lately. About you, Mom,

and me. Sometimes it helps, but sometimes it makes everything harder."

"Same here. What were you thinking about?"

"All kinds of things. That day at the beach when we ate those snow cones."

"Yeah, we all had neon blue tongues for hours afterward. It was a perfect day."

"It was. And the bike rides in the woods. And how you and Mom always let me win at Uno," she said, showing a hint of a grin.

"Yes, guilty as charged. You must have thought you were unbeatable. But no free ride with Scrabble, Jills. You're on your own for that."

"I know," she said, looking down at the jumble of tiles and wishing her life was in order—back to how it used to be. "Everything is a big mess."

"Not everything in life is supposed to make sense," her father said.

"I miss Mom."

"I miss her, too." He placed his hand on Jillian's.

They stared at each other for a while in the silence of the kitchen.

"Thanks for leaving me some of the rugelach," he said. "It tasted just like hers. She taught you well."

"I guess it was okay." She pictured Jack scowling over the plate.

"I have something to give you." He got up from the table and went straight to a roll-top desk in the living room.

He returned with a tattered spiral-bound notebook. *From the Kitchen of Joan Mermelstein. Welcome, Dear Friends. There's Plenty for All* was written in purple ink on its white cover. Jillian let out a gasp at the sight of the notebook—a ghost from the past flooding her with the sounds and smells of those early Saturday mornings in the kitchen with her mother. She pressed it to her heart, where she kept it for several minutes. The notebook held family recipes her mother had carefully written down on dog-eared pages dotted with stray batter and drips of apricot and poppy seed filling. Jillian didn't want to let the notebook go. It felt like hugging Mom again.

When Jillian finally laid it on the table, she recognized the gold glitter and pictures of unicorns she had glued to its front the day Joan of Hearts opened. She ran her fingers over her mother's flowing handwriting covering every lined page, whispering the names of her favorite cookies, breads, pastries, and pies they had baked together: Joan's Marvelous Mandelbrot, Glazed Lemon Babka, Krunch-Tastic Kichels, and, of course, her mother's Chocolate Rugelach—the very recipe she had used for the class party. Jillian read out loud a special note her mother had written on the inside front cover:

To my dearest pâtissier,
What shall we bake together today?
Whatever you choose, I'll be with you . . . always.
Love,
Mom

"I know it's been hard thinking about baking without her," her father said, "but she asked me to give this to you when I thought you were ready to bake again. Since you made . . ."

"I wasn't quite ready," Jillian said. "But Grandma Rita started putting out ingredients . . ."

"And you didn't want the fire department here again."

"Yes," she said, smiling.

"Let's finish this Scrabble game before I nod off," her father said. "You know that you're allowed to take seven new tiles for your next turn. It's in the rules. You can always start with a fresh set of letters."

And so she did.

Chapter 7

For Jack, winter break meant more time to bake. He experimented with new flavor combinations, mixing crystallized ginger with hazelnuts, pumpkin spice with lavender, lemon zest with espresso. Zombie Brunch blared from speakers in the kitchen as he imagined himself competing in the Bakerstown Bonanza. In his wildest visions, Jack stood before Phineas Farnsworth III as his idol announced the winning dessert:

"Never in the history of this competition have I tasted anything so . . . so . . . I don't even think there's a proper word for it. I'll have to make one up . . . so *delicioscrumptious*! Of course I'm talking about Jack Fineman's tiramisu toffee trifle—this year's undisputed Bakerstown Bonanza winner! Jack, come up here. Everyone else can go home now!"

In Jack's mind, streamers and a zillion balloons rained down upon him as he was presented with a treasure trove of prizes: a $150,000 check, a lifetime supply of ingredients, every kitchen gadget made by Farnsworth's company, and an interview in *Chef's Monthly* magazine.

But the best part was yet to come. His winning recipe would also be the featured dessert in the *Farnsworth Best of the Bonanza*, the annual cookbook containing the top contestants' recipes. It had been published every year since the first event in 1944. To Jack, having his pastry displayed on the cover would be his ticket to fame. It was more important to him than the money, the gadgets, and all the free sugar in the world. A recipe with his name on the cover of the *Farnsworth Best of the Bonanza* would last *forever.*

Only one small detail stood in the way of Jack's dream. The contest rules stated participants had to be at least eighteen years old. In the meantime, Jack studied his collection of all seventy-four editions of the *Farnsworth Best of the Bonanza* like an anthropologist examines artifacts pulled from ancient ruins. He crammed the pages of his scrapbook with notes about every winning recipe, looking for ideas to help him once he was picked.

Bruce wants to win the British Open. Chad dreams of riding his snowboard in the X Games. Me? I'm going to win the Bakerstown Bonanza . . . someday.

Sitting on the sofa, Jack reread the article from *The Ardmore Star* about the first baking contest held during the Ardmore County Fair in the Culinary Arts Pavilion. The event was the brainchild of Phineas Farnsworth, founder of the Farnsworth Baking Supply Company and the grandfather of Farnsworth III. A dozen women wearing identical checkered aprons and brown hairnets baked their favorite desserts using Farnsworth sugar and the company's new mixing bowls. The winner, Edna Harberg from nearby Warsaw, Ohio, received a crisp $100 bill and a fifty-pound sack of sugar. According to the article, Phineas Farnsworth called her rhubarb pie "blissfully divine."

The next year, thirty bakers participated and the attendance tripled. As the Farnsworth baking empire expanded, so did the contest. By the mid-1960s, thousands of people from around the country applied to be part of the "Nation's Most Popular Baking Challenge," as company brochures for the event bragged. Newspapers and women's magazines covered the spectacle like it was the World Series. When the Bakerstown Bonanza grew too big for the fairgrounds, it was moved to the Samuel P. Ardmore Convention Center. The building's auditorium could hold ten thousand people. Every seat was always filled.

At the age of four, Jack attended his first Bonanza, squeezing between rows of attendees to snag a spot where he could get a clear view of Farnsworth III, who took bites of each dessert before offering his opinions into a microphone.

From then on, Jack assumed the same position—front and center—mesmerized by the proceedings and eyeing each contestant for secrets. His favorite was George

Erdmeyer, who dominated the competition with a five-layer pineapple torte with swirls of macadamia nut cream running throughout the lofty dessert. After winning the contest, Erdmeyer, a school janitor from McCutchenville, Montana, hosted his own cooking show, *By George, Let's Bake*, on the Fab Food Network.

Jack closed the scrapbook and wrote down a story problem: *Jack is eleven years old. Contestants must be at least eighteen. How many days must Jack wait to win the Bakerstown Bonanza?*

He subtracted 11 from 18 and multiplied the remainder (7) by the number of days in a year (365). He buried his face in his hands at the sight of the answer.

"2,555 days," he groaned. "A long 2,555 days."

Chapter 8

As Jack entered homeroom after winter break, the word "rugelach" leaped to the front burner of his mind.

Jack glanced at Jillian. After looking through his baking scrapbook and watching past competitions on YouTube, he had come up with another theory as to why she couldn't possibly have made the rugelach.

Why didn't Jillian come forward and say so? Why make it if no one knows it was you? It's like telling the world's funniest joke to an empty room. What's the point?

Jillian looked straight ahead. She echoed Grandma Rita's reason why Jack had disliked her holiday offering: *That boy wouldn't know a decent rugelach if it jumped up and bit him in the tuchus!*

"Okay, class. Time to get back to work," Ms. Riedel said after the morning announcements. She wrote the word "entomology" on the chalkboard. "Does anyone know what this means?"

Jillian did but kept quiet. After the holiday party, she vowed that her days of getting noticed in class were over.

Chad cautiously raised his right hand.

"Uh, would that be the study of pastries?"

"Excuse me?" Ms. Riedel said.

"Like Entenmann's. Entomology is the study of Entenmann's, right? Their cheese Danish rules."

The class tittered.

Jack shook his head, knowing that Chad wasn't making a joke.

Not only can't Jack judge a rugelach, but he also has a questionable choice of friends, Jillian thought.

Jack raised his hand. "It's the study of insects," he said.

"Bingo," Ms. Riedel said.

"Wow, look who got a dictionary for Hanukkah," Chad mumbled.

"Our next unit will be about the endlessly fascinating world of bugs," Ms. Riedel continued. "Grasshoppers, ants, walking sticks, bees, fireflies. You name it, we're going to study it! Creeping, flying, biting, stinging, burrowing, the whole nine yards."

Jillian perked up. She had spent hours with her mother and father in their urban garden inspecting insects of all kinds. One year they watched as tiny praying mantises hatched out of an egg sac. Another time while visiting Grandma Rita, they saw red-eyed cicadas crawl out of the ground behind her petunia bed.

"These are seventeen-year cicadas," her mother had told her. "We visited here the last time they came up, way before you were born. They were buzzing everywhere. We won't see them again until you're twenty-two years old. That's because they live underground for seventeen years. Imagine that!"

Jillian watched her classmates. She noticed several students looked ill.

Victims of entomophobia, fear of insects. Or in Chad's case, fear of baked goods.

"And we'll be studying spiders, too," Ms. Riedel said. "They're arachnids, which have eight legs and two main body parts. Insects have six legs and three main body parts."

A chorus of "ewww" erupted. Ms. Riedel pressed on.

"A spider's body is covered with a cuticle, a hard outer shell that the spider sheds from time to time. When it forms a new cuticle, the old one cracks and the spider climbs out with a soft, brand-new skin."

Cool, Jillian thought.

"We're often scared of things we don't understand," Ms. Riedel said. "Consider this a chance to embrace and overcome your fears. Plus, there are way more insects than humans. The ratio is about two hundred million to one, so you might as well get to know your neighbors."

Awesome, Jack thought, feeling slightly guilty for all the mosquitoes he had swatted last summer.

"Next Monday, you will do group presentations. I want you to be creative. Use your talents. For example, act out how bees behave in a hive. Write poems about butterflies. Put on a play about Goliath beetles in the Amazon rain forest. It's up to *you*."

Now Jillian felt ill. She was fine with the creative part. Working in a group with kids she barely knew—and didn't want to know—would be worse than jostling a hornet's nest.

"As part of Mix-It-Up Month, I've divided the class into groups of three. I jumbled your names using an app on my phone. There will be no switching and no arguments."

Ms. Riedel handed out project folders with names written in black marker on the front.

"You have thirty minutes to discuss your projects before our math lesson."

Jillian looked at her folder. The cover showed her name and two others: Jack Fineman and Chad Albertson. She knew exactly what she wished to do for the project. She wanted to turn into a seventeen-year cicada.

Chad and Jack sat next to Jillian in the back corner of the room. All Jillian could think about was Jack and the rugelach. All Jack could think about was Jillian and the rugelach. They had *nothing* to say to each other. After three minutes, Chad could no longer stand the silence.

"Okay, let me get this out of the way. I'm *not* doing an interpretive beehive dance. Not gonna happen."

"Me neither," Jack agreed. "Something like that goes viral and, boom, your life is over."

"Or poems, like 'An Ode to an Earwig,'" Chad continued. "Won't do it."

"Right with you, bro," Jack said.

For the next five minutes, Jack and Chad rattled off a list of things they would *not* do: singing, acting, dancing, or anything involving puppets.

Jillian had heard enough.

"This is getting us nowhere," she said. "Is there something you *will* do?"

Jack and Chad were taken aback by the forceful sound of Jillian's voice. It wasn't the whisper they had heard at the holiday party.

I will not get an F on the project because you guys can't make up your minds, she thought.

"I suppose you have an idea," Chad shot back. "I know, why don't you make rugensplock—or whatever it is—with bugs in it."

This time Chad *was* kidding.

"That's it!" Jack said, nearly tumbling out of his chair.

45

"Let's do our project on insects as food. Lots of great chefs use bugs in their recipes."

"You'll get us expelled," Chad said.

"No, wait! Hear me out! Cultures all over the world eat bugs—lots of them. Wax worms, grasshoppers, ants, katydids, dragonflies. They're high in protein. And I bet they would make a cookie crunch."

"Entomophagy," Jillian said.

"What?" Chad asked. "I'm assuming that has nothing to do with crumb cake."

"Entomophagy means humans eating insects," she said.

"Did you borrow Jack's new dictionary?"

Jack held up his phone. "Look, here's a recipe for Chocolate Chirp Cookies with roasted crickets and honey."

"I'm not sure I'm good with this," Chad whined as the Twinkie and root beer he had consumed for breakfast did somersaults in his stomach.

"This is a chance to embrace your fears," Jack said.

"Yeah, but bugs in cookies . . ."

"You can always do the beehive dance instead, Chad," Jillian said.

"Fine, I'm in," Chad groaned, slouching in the chair.

"So it's settled," Jack said. "Let's meet at my house on Sunday to work on our project."

Then I'll know once and for all if Jillian knows her way around a kitchen.

At home in bed that night, Jillian flipped through her mother's notebook and scanned the page of the chocolate rugelach recipe. There were special notes written up and down each side. Jillian recited them out loud:

"On a bad day, add an extra bar of chocolate."

"What's better than a batch of chocolate rugelach? A double batch, of course!"

"Dough should be properly chilled. So just chill, okay?"

"Be flaky. If it's right for the rugelach, it's right for you!"

"To make a good rugelach, you gotta learn to roll with it."

"The filling is the heart of the rugelach. So give it your heart."

This last note took Jillian back to Joan of Hearts Pastry Shop when she was seven, making rugelach for the first time.

After kneading the dough into a rectangle, Jillian cut it into four sections, put them in a plastic bag, and set it in the refrigerator.

"Now we wait for the dough to chill. Can you guess what's next?" her mother asked.

"The chocolate?"

"Yes."

She handed Jillian two bars of semisweet chocolate. Jillian placed them in a double boiler on the stove. A low flame licked the bottom of the pan as she dropped in two tablespoons of butter and sprinkled in cocoa and cinnamon.

"Now stir gently until it's completely melted. Take your time. That's right. Now add the sugar and the salt. Then mix."

"Salt? I don't want the rugelach to be salty! It should be sweet."

"Jilly, it takes all kinds of flavors to make rugelach. Salt can be too salty and sugar too sweet. But blend them together and you get . . ."

"Magic!"

"You're a fast learner, Jilly."

Chapter 9

Jack texted Chad and Jillian:

Jack

Can't wait to bake with bugs! Bring any cooking gadgets you'll need.

Chad

Did you get the crickets?

Jack

Yep. A whole bagful online. I also found a recipe for oatmeal cricket cookies.

Jillian

I'll be there.

Chad

Can't I just Skype while you cook?

Jack

No way! You need to participate.

Jillian

Two words—beehive dance.

Chad

See you there.

Loud rock music blared from Jack's record player as Jillian and Chad entered the kitchen. It was the third track from the Zombie Brunch album:

> *Yeah, yeah, yeah, yeah, yeah, yeah, yeah!*
> *My favorite word, can you guess?*
> *Yeah, yeah, yeah, yeah, yeah, yeah, yeah!*
> *It's how us zombies all say, Yeeeeesssss!*

Chad clutched a bottle of antacid tablets. Jillian brought a CD of *The Four Seasons* and her mother's wooden spoon. Hearing the music and seeing all the contraptions Jack had laid out, Jillian wondered why she had bothered. The countertop was littered with several shiny objects she had never seen before.

"What's this?" she shouted over the throbbing bass.

"That's an Xtreme Adjustable Level Measuring Spoon," Jack said, turning down the volume. "Its built-in lever moves up and down so you can trim off excess ingredients.

50

It's part of the Phineas Farnsworth III Kitchen Genius Collection. See, there are his initials, PF, on the handle. I read that he has a huge private laboratory where he works on his gadgets. Pretty cool, huh?"

Jillian nodded politely.

I'll keep my old measuring cups and spoons, thank you very much, she thought. *And who's this Phineas Farnsworth guy?*

"And this is an EZ One-Click Butterizer, another of his creations. You load a stick of butter in this box, press a button, and *voilà,* a perfect slice every time without the mess! What else would you use?"

Hmmm, that's a hard one. Let me see . . . maybe a knife?

Jack looked at the worn wooden spoon in Jillian's hand. It was the kind of evidence he had hoped for.

I present to you Exhibit A—an old wooden spoon. Jillian Mermelstein is not the rugelach-maker. Not by a long shot.

"Nobody's bigger in baking than Phineas Farnsworth III. Someday I'm going to be just as famous as him," Jack said. "And I'm going to win the Bakerstown Bonanza— the world's biggest baking contest! It's held every year in Ardmore, but you probably already know that."

Jillian shrugged.

"Can we hurry?" Chad begged. "I'd like to get this over with as soon as possible."

The three went to work measuring ingredients

and following the steps to make the batter. Over Jack's objections, Jillian insisted that she stir it with the wooden spoon.

"This would go a lot faster if we used my Farnsworth two-hundred-watt chrome-plated mixer with self-cleaning, heat-treated beaters!"

Patience, Jillian thought. *Cooking is a prayer whispered . . .*

Jillian looked up to see a tall boy holding a putter. He wore peach-and-maroon-checkered slacks and a black polo shirt. Jack had forgotten that Bruce would be in charge tonight since their parents were attending a hospital fundraiser.

"Yuck, yuck, and triple yuck," Bruce said, looking into the bowl. "I wouldn't eat that if you paid me a million dollars. How are you planning on ruining this? With lime juice, asparagus, and pinto beans?"

Bruce turned to Jillian and Chad.

"I have to live with the Feebler Elf, so let me give you some advice. Stop hanging out with him before he infects you with his ridiculous dream of becoming a great pastry chef. Listen up! It . . . is . . . a . . . complete . . . waste . . . of . . . time!"

Before anyone could respond, Bruce disappeared into his room to practice putting.

Trying to think of a clever comeback on the fly, Chad shouted at him from the kitchen, "Oh, yeah,

Mr. Checkered-Pants-Golfing-Stupid-Guy, we'll see about that. Jack is the best!"

"Good one," Jack said, shaking his head.

I'm so glad I'm an only child, Jillian thought.

"Sorry about that," Jack said. "My brother is, uh, kind of a jerk."

"Come on. It's getting late," Jillian said. "Let's put in the roasted crickets."

Jack pulled the bag from his backpack. The label read: *Crunchy Critters, Wingless Whole Roasted Crickets, Plain.* Through the clear cellophane, the brownish insects were tangled in a pile of eyes, legs, thoraxes, and abdomens.

"They also come in flavors like barbecue, honey mustard, cinnamon and spice, and ranch jalapeño," Jack said, taking one out to inspect it.

Chad chomped two antacid tablets. He dashed from the kitchen, dove onto the living room sofa, and hugged one of the cushions.

Jillian dumped a cupful of crickets into the bowl and stirred until they were coated with the oatmeal batter. Together, she and Jack placed spoonfuls of dough onto cookie sheets, making sure each dollop contained at least three bugs. Once the cookies had baked for fifteen minutes, they placed them on cooling racks. Other than the appearance of a stray leg, they resembled normal oatmeal raisin cookies.

Jillian admitted to herself that the baking session had

gone better than expected despite Jack's brother, Zombie Brunch, and the countless times the Bakerstown Bonanza and Phineas Farnsworth III's name were mentioned.

"Ready for a taste test?" Jack asked.

"Two billion people around the world eat bugs," Jillian said, taking a nibble and chewing slowly. "Now make that two billion and one."

"Two billion and two," Jack said, shoving an entire cookie into his mouth. "Not bad. The crickets have a solid crunch that complements the soft oatmeal. What's your take?"

Knowing this was no ordinary cookie, Jack wanted to shout like he was one year old again, "Yum! More! Now!"

I should have tried crickets a long time ago, he thought.

Jillian didn't want Jack to know she was a foodie like him. It would lead to too many questions.

"It was okay," she said.

"Just *okay*?"

What Jillian wanted to say: *Well, when cooked, the crickets have a soy texture that I like, but the cinnamon overpowers the taste. I'd have scaled back a tad on the cinnamon or used cayenne pepper in its place. Also, a higher grade of oats would have enhanced the experience, along with a bit less butter.*

This is what she *did* say: "Yeah, they were a little chewy."

"I see," Jack replied.

After Jillian and Chad left, Jack arranged the cricket-filled cookies on a large plate, covered them with foil, and set them on the middle shelf of the refrigerator. On a sticky note, he drew a skull and crossbones above the words, *WARNING!!! DO NOT EAT!!! CLASS PROJECT FOR TOMORROW!!!* Just in case Mom and Dad were hungry when they came home.

"Good night, my little six-legged friends," Jack said, closing the door. "See you soon. *Chirp. Chirp.*"

Chapter 10

Jack woke up early so he could prepare for the presentation. He decided to surprise Jillian and Chad by dressing like Farnsworth, who was never seen in public without a three-piece suit, a silk tie, and expensive polished shoes. As he finished gluing on a fake goatee and putting on a red beret, he heard a rustling noise in the kitchen, like a burglar rummaging through a dresser drawer.

In the refrigerator's dim light, Jack's eyes caught a flash of checkered periwinkle and pink. He moved closer to see Bruce's angular profile bent inside the open refrigerator.

Bologna? For breakfast? You are *hopeless.*

Then he heard grotesque gobbling noises—the kind reserved for flesh-eating monster movies. Sandy-colored crumbs speckled with flecks of brown rained down around Bruce's sneakers. Jack tried to shout but could only manage a garbled, "Bruce . . . stop . . ."

In horror, his brother turned around. The foil had been flung aside. Half the cookies were gone.

"I couldn't help myself," Bruce said, breathlessly. "I thought I'd take just one bite to see how awful they were. But they were good. Unbelievably good. Out-of-this-world goooood."

Jack swelled with pride. This was the first time Bruce had *ever* eaten anything he had made.

I finally conquered the fussiest eater in all of Ardmore!

"It must have been something that girl did because there's no way you could have made oatmeal raisin cookies this delicious. Not . . . a . . . chance."

"Oh," Jack sighed, bowing his head. "But Bruce, those aren't raisins . . ."

"Sorry, no more time to talk, Duncan Heinie. I've got to get ready for school. You better clean up this mess before Mom comes down."

Bruce went into the bathroom to brush his teeth. Smiling in the mirror, he saw what appeared to be spiny dark splinters stuck between his teeth. Looking closer, he screamed.

Arriving ten minutes late, Jack rushed into homeroom where Chad and Jillian were waiting impatiently.

"What happened, man?" Chad asked. "Our presentation is first. Ms. Riedel said we'd have to give it without you if you didn't show."

"Half the cookies are gone," Jack said, pulling back the ripped foil to reveal stray cricket parts.

Jillian gazed at the plate. "What happened?"

"Bruce ate them."

"Bruce? Your brother?" Chad asked. "Mr. Checkered-Pants-Golfing-Stupid-Guy ate our cookies?"

"At first he couldn't resist them, but when he found crickets inside, he ran around the house shouting something about turning into a bug."

"Whoa, that would definitely hurt his golf game," Chad said, laughing. "In today's sports news, Bruce Fineman lost the Masters when his caddie accidentally squished him on the fifth green."

Jillian pictured Bruce as a flying insect clad in checkered pants and driving a golf cart. From deep within, she felt an unfamiliar sensation—a feeling buried inside for so long that she had forgotten it was even there, that it would ever be possible to experience again.

It was laughter . . . and there was no stopping it.

"Okay, class," Ms. Riedel said. "Jack, Jillian, and Chad will now present their topic, 'Incredible Edible Insects.'"

Jillian read a few of the slides from their PowerPoint presentation:

- There are over 1,900 types of edible bugs.
- Each one of you eats two pounds of bugs a year without knowing it.
- In some countries, ninety-six tons of caterpillars are eaten annually.
- Cockroaches have fifteen percent more protein in them than beef.
- Restaurants around the globe serve grasshoppers, ants, mealworms, and cricket-based dishes, including salads, soups, tacos, and even . . .

Jillian couldn't say the word. Her face turned red as she tried to mumble "cookies." All she saw was Bruce as a cricket sprouting wings and an antenna.

Shocked classmates stared as the girl from the back row laughed so hard tears streamed down her face. Jack joined her. Soon Chad was howling at a joke only the three of them understood.

"Great, how am I going to hit this golf ball with my compound eye!" Chad giggled. "I see thousands of them!"

Ms. Riedel stood back and watched. She knew about Jillian's background, the pastry shop, her mother's death, and her move to Ardmore. Putting her with Jack and Chad, two of Sieberling's biggest goofballs, hadn't been a random choice of her phone app. She had grouped them together hoping for this very response.

The three managed to stumble through to the end. Jack

offered the cookies to the class. A few brave souls tried them, but most refused to join the world's two-billion-and-two-bug-eater-club.

Jillian handed the plate to Chad.

"Embrace your fears," she said.

Chad held a cookie inches from his open mouth. For him, this was much harder than snowboarding down a fifty-four degree Alaskan incline, something he dreamed about all the time. Finally, he bit into it with a satisfying crunch.

Bruce was right.

"This is fantastic!" Chad said, removing an antenna wedged between his lower incisors.

During the next presentation, Jack asked Chad, "Was the cricket cookie as good as the rugelach?"

"Yes," he admitted. "They were both incredible. I only told you the rugelach was 'okay' because I didn't want to hurt your feelings. Sorry, bro. I have to be straight with you. Jillian can really bake. Uh, not as good as you of course, I mean . . ."

"Thanks, Chad. Thanks a lot."

Jillian arrived home to find Grandma Rita at the kitchen table. Still thinking about Jack, Chad, Bruce, and the half-eaten plate of cricket cookies, she couldn't wait to talk about her unexpectedly hilarious day.

"Hey, Jilly, why don't you come sit with me? I have something to tell you."

From her somber expression, Jillian knew it was not good news.

"Your father is a good man, a proud man. He could never tell you this himself."

"Is he sick? Did he get hurt?" Jillian was starting to panic. What was Grandma Rita trying to say?

"No, he's fine, but he lost his proofreading job a while back and they cut his hours at the auto parts warehouse."

The news stunned Jillian. She thought her father was paying off their debts so they could move into their own place.

"I know you two want to find a house for yourselves and get on with your lives. It just looks like it may take a while longer. No matter what, we're all together as a family. That's what's important. And you'll always have a place to stay with me, if that's okay with you."

"Of course it is. We love it here, Grandma."

"You're sweet, Jilly, just like your mother. How about we do something nice for your father?"

"Like what?"

"Make a cake. It might cheer him up a bit."

"Let's make oatmeal raisin cookies instead," Jillian said, letting out a burst of laughter.

"What am I missing?"

"Get the mixing bowl. I've got a good story to tell you."

Chapter 11

As Jack settled in to watch television that night, he reviewed the events of the day. In his baking scrapbook he wrote:

Ms. Riedel gave us an A on our presentation! She said the cookie was scrumptious!

Bruce got in trouble for eating half of our project and leaving the kitchen a mess. No golf for a week!

Mom and Dad punished me for bringing roasted crickets into the house without permission. No cooking for two weeks!

Bruce ate about twenty bugs. Two weeks off from cooking? Totally worth it!

Chad ate three cricket cookies. He may turn into a foodie yet.

Jillian laughed . . . a lot.

EVERYONE, even Bruce, loved the cookies. Was it something Jillian did?

Jack paused and reread his last line.

Jillian brought a wooden spoon. When asked about the oatmeal cookie, her only comment was that it was "a little chewy."

"Definitely not foodie talk," Jack muttered to himself. *No matter what Chad or my brother may think, it still doesn't seem possible that Jillian made the rugelach,* he thought. *But she was fun to hang out with.*

Jack turned to a blank page and pasted in an advertisement for Farnsworth's latest cooking spray: *It's quick, it's slick, and your scones won't stick!* the headline read. Jack made a note to run out and buy a can.

Remote in hand, he scanned the television for cooking shows. He bounced between *In Crust We Trust,* a pie-making challenge hosted by the French pastry chef Francois Furveau; *Beasts of Yeast,* a competition for bread bakers from around the world; and *Shoot for the Spoon,* a show in which cooks had sixty minutes to make soup out of random ingredients pulled from a shopping cart while blindfolded. Jack stopped surfing when he saw a familiar face on the local evening news.

A reporter was interviewing Phineas Farnsworth III, who sat behind a large oak desk. He wore his signature pinstriped suit and a scowl that said, *You, my friend, are not worth the ground on which I walk.* Framed covers of his annual cookbook hung on the wall behind him.

This must be inside the Farnsworth mansion, Jack thought.

"So, Mr. Farnsworth, Channel 25 News has learned you have big plans for the Bakerstown Bonanza this year. Tell us about it."

Farnsworth cleared his throat.

"As you know, the Farnsworth Baking Supply Company has been sponsoring the Bonanza for seventy-four years. We've kept the competition the same from its inception. The prizes may have grown, but it's still a simple test of who can make the most delicious dessert—one worthy of carrying the Farnsworth name. It's about real people with real stories. There are no weird challenges or overrated celebrity chefs barking out commands: 'You have three minutes . . . now incorporate bacon into your raspberry strudel!' What a bunch of nonsense."

The reporter nodded, hesitant to interrupt. "So what changes will happen this year?"

"The rules will stay the same. They worked for my grandfather, they worked for my father—may they both rest in peace—and they work for me."

"Then what are the 'big plans' for this year?" the reporter asked, bracing for another gust of wind from Farnsworth.

"To celebrate our seventy-fifth year, we'll be featuring

the next generation of great chefs selected from the young people of Ardmore, Ohio."

Jack couldn't breathe.

"Starting immediately, I'll be accepting applications from bakers between the ages of eleven and thirteen. Two students from each eligible school in Ardmore will be chosen."

"And what will the first-place winners take home?"

Farnsworth looked directly into the camera, as if addressing Jack face-to-face.

"Oh, there's prize money, of course. Plus, the winning school will receive a nice surprise. But those things don't compare to the real reward."

"And that is . . . ?"

"Fame, you dimwit! Immortality! The chance to change your life forever. Halley's Comet comes around about every seventy-five years. For six youngsters out there, this will be their moment—their personal Halley's Comet."

"I see. How can they enter?"

"By going to our website. They can read the complete rules and download the application."

Jack shrieked so loudly his parents came running.

"What's wrong?" Mr. Fineman asked.

Unable to speak, Jack pointed to the television.

"I can enter the Bakerstown Bonanza this year!" Jack gasped. "I . . . can . . . enter . . . the Bonanza!"

"Settle down, Jack," Mr. Fineman said, sitting next to

him on the sofa. "Your mother and I have been talking about this baking thing."

Jack knew what was coming. He had been hearing the same lecture since third grade when he begged for a set of expensive Farnsworth Teflon frying pans for Hanukkah, the ones with "three-ply bonded construction and contoured stainless steel handles."

"It's not a *thing*, Dad. This means *everything* to me," Jack said. "You don't understand!"

"And that's the problem—this obsession of yours," Mrs. Fineman said. "We wish you'd concentrate on bringing up your grades instead. I would have never made it into medical school with your marks."

This wasn't the first time Jack's parents had questioned his lifelong plan to dominate the pastry world.

"There's nothing wrong with baking as a hobby," Mr. Fineman explained, glancing at one of the detailed pages of Jack's scrapbook. "But you have to be realistic. More practical."

"I'll work harder. Promise!" Jack said. "I'll do anything to be in the Bonanza."

"We know you'll do anything," Mrs. Fineman said. "And that's the problem. I'd rather we, I mean *you*, didn't have anything to do with the Farnsworth family. Nothing good will come of it."

"But this is my chance—my Halley's Comet!"

"We know this is your dream, Jack," Mrs. Fineman said.

"And we want to support you, just like we do with Bruce and his golfing . . ."

"And his pants?" Jack shot back.

"I assure you that Bruce is responsible for buying his own sportswear . . . and for his fashion decisions," Mr. Fineman said.

"You just don't think I'm good enough," Jack argued.

"Oh, you're good, Jack," Mrs. Fineman said. "As good as the best baker I've ever known, Leah Goldfarb."

"Is she on the Fab Food Network?"

"No," she continued. "But that's a story for another time. What we're trying to say is that life is more complicated than making cookies and winning baking prizes. We're sorry. Sometimes parents have to make tough decisions. This is one of those times."

"But . . ."

"There is also the issue of your last report card. We'll discuss the contest later," Mr. Fineman said.

Which means never, Jack thought.

News of the kids-only version of the annual baking contest spread quickly. Grandma Rita saw the article splashed across the front page of *The Ardmore Star.* The headline read: *Local Kids Get Taste of Fame.*

"Hey, Jills, did you know they're featuring students in this year's Bakerstown Bonanza?"

"No, I didn't. Who is Phineas Farnsworth III, anyway?

Jack had a lot of his kitchen gadgets. He wouldn't stop talking about him."

"He's the owner of the Farnsworth Baking Supply Company—the biggest employer in the city. He's easily the richest person in town, though I'm told he rarely visits here anymore. Spends most of the time at his chalet in Switzerland."

Grandma Rita handed the article to Jillian:

ARDMORE, OH—Business mogul and Ardmore native Phineas Farnsworth III is searching for six local children to be contestants in the 75th edition of the Bakerstown Bonanza. This first-ever version will highlight aspiring young pastry chefs from Ardmore competing to create this year's top dessert.

"From our research, we know many young people attend this event," said Farnsworth through a press release. "This is an opportunity to reach the chefs of tomorrow. It's also another way for the Farnsworth Baking Supply Company to give back to the city we love."

The article continued with a lengthy description of Farnsworth's international food empire.

"This guy sure is full of himself," Jillian said before continuing to read aloud.

"From the beginning, we've always kept the event in Ardmore—a town that represents the heart of America," Farnsworth said. "It's a place that literally smells of cinnamon rolls and fresh-baked apple pie. That's what my company's contest is all about, families and food."

"Give . . . me . . . a . . . break!" Jillian muttered.

"As usual, the event will take place the same weekend as the Ardmore Heritage Day Festival in May. To be considered, entrants, ages eleven through thirteen, must complete an application form, provide proof of residency, submit a five-minute video displaying a mastery of cooking skills, and write an essay on why they want to compete in the Bonanza."

"This sounds like homework to me. No, thanks." Jillian put down the newspaper at the sound of her father shuffling into the kitchen.

"Morning, Jills," Mr. Mermelstein said. "Be sure to save the crossword puzzle so we can do it together when I come home from work."

"Sure, Dad."

He's usually asleep before we get to the first clue.

Jillian's father spoke softly into Grandma Rita's ear before heading toward the door. A look of worry filled her face. He was about to leave when she said, "Walter, I need to have a word with you."

Jillian watched as her father and grandmother spoke in hushed tones from across the room. When their discussion ended, they approached Jillian together.

"Sometimes I need to be reminded that keeping secrets from my daughter isn't the right thing to do," Mr. Mermelstein said to Jillian. "After all, you're eleven years old. You deserve to know what's going on, right?"

Jillian nodded. "Is this about money?" she asked.

Mr. Mermelstein glared at Grandma Rita.

"So maybe we've talked about these things already . . . a little," Grandma Rita said, shrugging.

"It's okay, Dad. I want to know. I need to know. Please tell me."

"We've all been through a lot. And I've never been good with difficult news, so I'll get right to it. They let me go from my night job. It wasn't anything I did. The owner said he just didn't have enough work for me. Unfortunately, life can be a bit like Scrabble. You have to deal with the letters you get. Right now, the letters aren't so great. Does that make sense?"

Jillian thought about the mixed-up mess of letters she had recently pulled from the bag. She knew what her dad meant, but Scrabble was just a board game. This was real life. She was determined not to let him see how much the news bothered her.

"Yes, I see," she said. "You've got a rack full of vowels— all E's, I's, O's, A's, and U's—each worth one point. It's hard to make a high score with that. But you can always start with a fresh set of letters."

Mr. Mermelstein hugged Jillian. "Thank you for understanding. So smart, like your mother."

"Is there any way I can help?"

"Just keep working hard in school. We're going to be okay. Don't you worry."

"Where are you going now?"

"I found a part-time job filling potholes for the city. It's good work. Hard work, but good. And if I don't leave right now, I'll be late."

He said goodbye and walked out the door. Jillian heard the sound of his car backing out of the driveway and heading toward downtown.

When he was out of sight, Jillian went back to reading the article.

A boy and girl from Sieberling School, Old Harbor Academy, and Feldspar Math and Science Institute will be selected to compete in two-chef teams. The winning school will receive a deluxe, state-of-the-art Culinary Education Center underwritten by the Farnsworth Family Trust, featuring sixteen stainless steel kitchen units along with a 75-year supply of ingredients and baking tools.

The winning recipe will be highlighted on the cover of the anniversary edition of the *Farnsworth Best of the Bonanza* cookbook, which will include favorite desserts from past contests.

Big whoop, Jillian thought.

Finally, the top team will split a prize of $150,000.

Jillian dropped the paper.

"What's up, Jillian?" Grandma Rita asked. "I thought we were going grocery shopping."

"The groceries can wait!"

"Why?"

"Because I need to apply for the Bakerstown Bonanza—now!" Jillian called as she hurried to her room and pulled out her laptop.

Chapter 12

Jack downloaded the ten-page application form from the website. The questionnaire made it clear a parent or guardian must fill it out. In light of his parents' "get practical" lecture, Jack didn't bother asking. He feared they'd write something like:

Dear Mr. Farnsworth,

Here is our son's application. We filled it out because he won't stop annoying us about it. Please crush his dreams NOW so he can pursue something important, like becoming a brain surgeon or a certified public accountant. Thank you. BTW . . . we love your silicone muffin tins!

Jack wasn't going to take any chances. He'd been preparing for this moment all his life. Pretending to be his parents, he answered the questions himself.

How did your child learn to cook?

Jack taught himself. He has a natural gift. One of the first times he baked for his class (plum-filled cupcakes with cream cheese icing—his own creation), his teacher sent a note home calling him "a prodigy." Homeroom mothers and fathers bug him for his recipes all the time.

Has your child taken any cooking classes?

No. Why would he? He should be the one giving the lessons!

Who is your child's biggest influence?

Phineas Farnsworth III. He even has a life-size cutout of Farnsworth from a sugar display at our neighborhood Food Mart. He rescued it from a trash bin behind the store. Now it's in his room next to his bed.

What is your child's biggest strength in the kitchen? Do they have a secret weapon?

Jack knows the right ingredient to use in the right amount at the right time. He also knows a baker is only as good as his tools. He spends his allowance and birthday money buying every cooking gadget with Phineas Farnsworth's name on it.

What is your child's greatest weakness in the kitchen?

He makes other bakers look bad, but he can't help it.

Does your child have any other interests?

No. Baking is his life. He played in a soccer league once (our idea), but he kept running off the field to make sure the after-game snack he brought for the team (crème brûlée in Dixie cups) was properly chilled.

His only other hobby is collecting Farnsworth Best of the Bonanza cookbooks. He has all seventy-four editions, including the first one (a 1944 brochure with just a dozen recipes, signed by runner-up Gladys Zorn). The only one missing from his collection is the rare version of the 1983 book with a typo calling for one tablespoon of kosher "silt" rather than "salt" in champion Deloris Langston's apple dumpling recipe.

The final question was the biggie:

Why does your child want to compete in the Bakerstown Bonanza? (500 words or less)

Jack didn't need 500 words to answer this one.

For as long as we can remember, Jack's dream has been to win the Bonanza and to become as famous as Phineas Farnsworth III. Being crowned champion is part of his plan to be the best pastry chef who ever lived.

Jack reread his application and smiled.

This is perfect! *Now all I have to do is make the video, convince Mom or Dad to sign the release form, submit my entry, and wait for the news. A piece of cake!*

Jillian cringed as she scanned the list of questions on the application.

This is way too personal, she thought. *My biggest influence? How did I learn to cook? Can't we just bake? Why do they need to know so much about us?*

She flipped to the small print on the back page: *The Bakerstown Bonanza reserves the right to use all material provided to us by contestants at our own discretion in perpetuity.*

The word "discretion" gave her a bad feeling. The dictionary entry read: *Discretion—The freedom to decide what should be done in a particular situation.* Then she looked up "in perpetuity." It meant "forever."

That means they can take whatever I write down and use it in any way they please for as long as they want, Jillian thought. *It means sharing details about Mom, Dad, and the pastry shop.*

Before filling out another word, Jillian watched videos of past competitions. It turned out the event was about more than baking. Finalists were required to get in front of the microphone and answer questions from Farnsworth about their recipes. Contestants sometimes wept as they talked about the desserts they made. They openly shared family tragedies and discussed what they planned to do if they won the money. Jillian imagined the kids' version would be more of the same.

The thought that her family's private life would be on display for all of Ardmore to see made Jillian squirm. The idea that whatever she said and did would be captured on every phone and posted on social media made her nauseated.

Then Jillian watched the video of Farnsworth from the local evening news. She listened as he hurled insults at the reporter, never smiling once during the interview.

Jillian reread the final question on the application: *Why does your child want to compete in the Bakerstown Bonanza?*

On a scrap of notebook paper, she wrote her honest reply: *My mother died a year ago and left our family in debt. My father can't find steady work and we seriously need the money. If I win, I'll give my part of the money to Dad. Also, I miss Mom, but I know that winning this contest won't bring her back.*

Jillian didn't want to exploit her mother's death or

her family's financial problems to be in the Bonanza. But she was determined to win the prize money. She needed to come up with another story to convince Farnsworth to choose her as one of Sieberling School's two contestants.

So she lied.

ℭhapter 13

𝒥illian read her essay to Grandma Rita:

There is no one I know who cooks quite like Grandma Rita. My father calls what she makes "indescribable."

Once, she baked a blueberry pie and people from miles away showed up at her door. Her neighbors in Ardmore still talk about that blueberry pie and the unbelievable smell coming from the house. Mrs. Eberman, the lady who lives next door, tells me she will never forget it as long as she lives. Then she hugs me tight and sobs a little.

When my bubbe (that's Yiddish for "grandma") and I recently made chocolate rugelach in her kitchen, I carefully studied her every move. I watched her empty out the spice rack and the utensil drawer onto the counter. I saw how she blended the ingredients and prepared the oven. Everything she did was a new lesson for me. Often, she would sit back and say, "Jills, show me what you would do."

Cooking is only a small part of what makes Grandma Rita special. She's also a math professor, a plumber, an electrician, a mechanic, and a long-distance runner. In fact, if she never baked another thing in her life, that would be okay because there's so much more of her to love.

When we bake, she says it reminds her of the happiest moments of her life as a young mother. And that's the reason I want to be a contestant in the Bakerstown Bonanza. Because my grandmother says watching me bake helps her to remember and fills her with joy.

At first Grandma Rita laughed. By the end she was crying.

"Everything you wrote is technically true," she said. "Of course, the people who showed up at my door were firefighters. And yes, my cooking lessons usually demonstrate what *not* to do! How your mother ended up being such an amazing pastry chef is a mystery."

"Are you okay with it?" Jillian asked.

"Jills, of course I am. It's a beautiful essay. Whoever's picking the contestants will love the touching story of a Jewish grandmother baking with her granddaughter. But can I ask you a question?"

"Go ahead."

"Why not write about your mother? She was the real baker in the family."

"I've watched videos of past Bonanzas," Jillian said. "It's not something Mom would have ever been involved in."

"Yes, I remember: Cooking is not a contest. It is a prayer whispered humbly . . ."

"As the sun rises," Jillian continued. "When no one else is looking. During the Bonanza, the whole world will be looking. I've thought a lot about this. If I talk about Mom, about our baking, my memories of her will no longer belong to me . . . to us. They will belong to everyone . . . and anyone . . . for perpetuity. I don't want that to happen. And it will be just too painful to talk about, especially with everyone watching."

"I understand," Grandma Rita said. "But then the big question is: Do you really want to be in it?"

No. It goes against everything my mother taught me about baking . . . and about life.

"Yes, it's my chance to help out our family. I have to."

"Well, then, let's shoot your video and get you signed up."

That night in her room, Jillian wondered what her mother would have thought about her bending the truth, or applying for the contest in the first place. Looking through the recipe book, she traveled back to her first chocolate rugelach lesson.

"Get the dough out of the refrigerator," her mother said. "It's time to do some rolling! Did you know that rugelach means 'little twists' in Yiddish?"

Her mother instructed Jillian to take each of the four sections of dough and flatten them into circles about nine inches wide.

"Like a pizza," Jillian said.

"Precisely. Now put down a layer of the chocolate filling on each circle."

"Like this?" Jillian asked, dripping syrupy sweetness from her spoon onto each piece.

"You're doing a super job! Go ahead and cut the circles into eight triangular sections."

When Jillian finished the first circle, some of the triangles were fat and others were thin. Two of them didn't resemble a triangle at all.

"It's ruined!" Jillian cried. "I've ruined the rugelach!"

"On the contrary, your triangles are perfectly imperfect! Absolutely wonderful."

Starting at the wide end of the triangles, they took turns rolling the wedges of dough. When done, Jillian pouted.

"Look, Jillian. Each one is unique—flawed, oddly shaped, and curious. That's what makes them delightful."

"No, they're ugly!"

"How could anything made with love be ugly? You cut them exactly the way they were supposed to be."

"But I want them to be perfect."

"Perfection only comes when you realize that perfection is unattainable. Someday you will understand."

Jillian turned off the bedroom light and drifted to sleep, thinking about her grandmother's perfectly imperfect blueberry pie.

With Chad's help, Jack completed the five-minute video. Now, he faced one last hurdle: getting one of his parents to sign the application.

"I've been studying extra hard," Jack pleaded during dinner. "I got an A minus on my social studies quiz. I'll take out the garbage until I'm forty-five. Pleeeaaaasssse!"

Bruce remained silent, secretly plotting a way to get revenge for the "cricket calamity," as the incident had become known around the Fineman house.

"We'll see," Mrs. Fineman said.

"Look, I'll even eat my peas!"

"Jack, you always eat your peas," Mr. Fineman said. "You love peas. And Brussels sprouts and fried cabbage. That's not going to work."

Bracing himself for another buckle-down-at-school lecture, Jack brought the application paperwork to his father's study later that evening. Mr. Fineman took the questionnaire and read out loud:

Is there anyone else in your household who bakes?

No. Jack tried to teach us, but he gave up after one lesson. He said it was like trying to show an alpaca how to ice a Napoleon.

"An alpaca?" Mr. Fineman said. "What is that supposed to mean?"

"Well, an alpaca doesn't have an opposable thumb . . . " Jack began.

"We were supposed to write this, not you. I would never have said this."

"I thought I'd save you the trouble."

Mr. Fineman read further:

Does your child have a favorite pastry or cookie they recently prepared?

Jack's Oatmeal Cricket Cookies were delicious—a stunning combination of a traditional grain and chirping insect. His brother Bruce was crazy about them.

The more his father read, the more he became convinced there was little chance Farnsworth would pick Jack. So he signed the application.

When Mrs. Fineman found out, she was furious.

"I can't believe you let him enter!" she said. "You know how I feel about Phineas Farnsworth III. I'll never trust anything that man touches. What if Jack gets chosen?"

"I don't think you'll have to worry about that," Mr. Fineman said. "In the application, he mentioned the crickets."

"He did?"

"Yes."

"You're right. We don't have anything to worry about. But what if he *doesn't* get picked? Then his lifelong dream will be over. What will we say to him? He'll be devastated."

"I know. I guess this is what you call a no-win situation."

Chapter 14

ack had always been confident about his baking skills, but the days leading up to Farnsworth's announcement of who would be picked filled him with doubt. From the buzz around his homeroom and the cafeteria, Jack estimated that most of Ms. Riedel's sixth-grade class had applied to be contestants.

Jack dismissed the idea that Jillian had entered. After their class project, she returned to her seat in the back, where she remained quiet unless called upon. The girl who had laughed so hard about the cricket cookies didn't seem capable of even a faint smile now.

During the evening news, Farnsworth mentioned that the deadline for sending in applications had ended. The camera panned to a stack of papers reaching from the top of his desk to the top of his bald head.

"Well, young bakers of Ardmore, it looks like I've

got my work cut out for me," Farnsworth said. "It won't be easy whittling this down to only six contestants, I assure you."

The size of the stack staggered Jack. It never occurred to him so many kids in his hometown were interested in baking. And Ardmore was only one town in a state teeming with towns just like it—in a country with thousands of Ardmores and hundreds of thousands of kids like Jack. He would have to rise above the seven billion inhabitants of Earth to become the planet's top pastry chef. But first he had to rule his own little corner of the world.

Have my parents and Bruce been right all along? Maybe I am wasting my time.

Jillian also saw the mountain of applications on TV. She imagined countless other kids making rugelach, or macaroons, or paczkis with their grandmothers. Even in a town the size of Ardmore, she figured there were lots of kids like her with families who could use the prize money.

I'll probably get passed over. If so, I'll have to think of another way to help Dad.

Over the last few days, Jillian watched her father drag himself into the house. His hands and lips were cracked from the brutal cold. Last Sunday he had skipped their Scrabble game and fell straight into bed.

Jillian figured that if her father knew she was entering

the contest to help him with money, he might discourage her from applying. So, when she had handed him the forms, she told him it was a permission slip for a school field trip.

Her stomach clenched thinking about the lies that had begun to pile up.

Sorry, Mom, she thought. *I have to do this for the family. I know you would understand. I'm just being perfectly imperfect.*

Jack fidgeted in his chair. He doodled on his math quiz and repeatedly cracked his knuckles until there was no crack left. To his teacher's annoyance, he asked to go to the restroom three times before lunch.

"What's wrong with you, dude?" Chad asked.

"Farnsworth is announcing the contestants tonight. Channel 25 is running a special on the history of the Bonanza. And at the end of the show . . ." Jack trailed off, glancing at the clock. "Ugh, seven more hours of agony," he said.

"What's the worst thing that could happen?"

"I don't get picked."

"Nope, you're wrong. There's something worse. You don't get picked *and* Bruce forces you to wear his pair of lilac-and-jade pants. Oh, and then he attacks you with a pitching wedge."

Jack laughed. "Can you come over? I'm going to need someone rooting for me."

"I'll be there, Chef Fineman. And I won't let Mr. Checkered-Pants-Golfing-Stupid-Guy get you, either."

After dinner, Jack and his family gathered around the television. Bruce agreed to join them, certain he would be performing a victory dance when Jack's name wasn't called. His parents tried to get comfortable on their recliners, hoping for the best outcome, though they weren't entirely sure what that would be. Chad secretly brought a bag of blue and gold glitter and an air horn—the kind with explicit instructions saying, *Not for Indoor Use*.

Jack remained unusually quiet. His father kept glancing at his watch while his mother frowned every time Farnsworth appeared on the screen. Bruce pretended to ignore the show and practiced putting a golf ball across the living room into a glass lying on its side. The plinking sound was driving Jack nuts.

Finally, it was time. All eyes in the Finemans' living room turned to the towering man in the three-piece suit holding six pieces of paper.

"Before I begin, let me say, Ardmore, Ohio, you have done yourself proud," Farnsworth said. "As I had predicted, it was extremely difficult finding the best two candidates to represent each of the three schools in the Bakerstown Bonanza. There were many exceptional applications."

Mr. Fineman shot a nervous look at his wife.

"And now the finalists."

Jack leaned in.

"The team from Feldspar Math and Science Institute will be made up of twelve-year-old Quentin Lindenberg and thirteen-year-old Marcia Thorne." A short clip from each of their videos played, showing Quentin baking treats for his cats and rescue ferret, and Marcia decorating cakes for her one-year-old triplet brothers.

"Representing Old Harbor Academy will be twelve-year-old Veronica Hartman and eleven-year-old Reginald Nestland." Veronica's video showed her at the Ardmore Nursing Home giving a cooking class to the elderly residents. Reginald decorated the top of a cake with a lifelike portrait of Phineas Farnsworth III.

Jack tried to swallow. Bruce put down his club and practiced a jig. Chad clutched the bag of glitter and positioned his finger on the trigger of the air horn. Jack's parents gripped the arms of their recliners.

"And finally, the eleven-year-old bakers from Sieberling School are . . ."

Mr. and Mrs. Fineman reached out and grasped hands.

"Jillian Mermelstein and Jack Fineman."

Jack let out a piercing shriek five times louder than his yelp after first tasting solid food. Bruce covered his ears. Mr. and Mrs. Fineman nearly fainted, wondering how the cricket cookies had not instantly disqualified Jack from consideration.

"I knew it! I knew it! Farnsworth had to pick me! He just had to! BOOM!"

Chad unleashed the bag of glitter and blasted the air horn: *HOOONNNNK! HOOONNNNNNK!*

Jack paused to view Jillian's video clip, which showed her making rugelach with Grandma Rita and talking about her special wooden spoon.

Mr. Fineman watched in shock as his son's video played. Jack shouted out lyrics to a Zombie Brunch song and threw ingredients into his Farnsworth Deluxe 5000 Food Processor. The camera zoomed in. "Get a good look at the next big thing from Ardmore, folks! Remember the name—Jack Fineman. I rock! I rule! I am the king! Yeah, yeah, yeah, yeah, yeah, yeah, yeah!"

"Congratulations, Jack," Mr. Fineman said, vigorously patting him on the back and reminding him not to forget to finish his report on the Civil War. "Remember, it's due next week."

Mrs. Fineman gave her son a warm hug. "We hope this lives up to your dreams, Jack," she said. "We know this means a lot to you. Now go get 'em."

Sweat covering his forehead, Jack bounded around the room. Then it dawned on him. He finally had his answer about the chocolate rugelach.

Jillian made it! But she had help—her grandmother.

Jack was about to share this news with Chad when Mrs. Fineman thrust a vacuum cleaner into his hands. "We are

91

really proud of you," she said. "But before you celebrate anymore, I suggest you and your friend clean up every speck of this glitter. It's everywhere."

When Jillian and Grandma Rita heard Farnsworth's announcement, they fell into each other's arms and jumped up and down. Then they clinked glasses of sparkling grape juice that Grandma Rita had saved for the occasion.

"A toast to Jillian Mermelstein! You're going to be great!" Grandma Rita said. "I'm sure of it."

"But why . . . why would they put me with Jack Fineman?" Jillian asked. "We had fun doing the science project together, but did you see his video? We couldn't be more different in the kitchen."

"He's the cocky contestant—the one everyone wants to see go down in defeat. I've watched some of these cooking reality shows. They often pair a Jack with someone like you—the person everyone roots for. It makes for good drama and higher ratings."

"Then how am I going to win? We're on a team!"

"Maybe the answer is in your mother's recipe book."

Chapter 15

When Jack and Jillian arrived at school the next day, their classmates froze as if a pair of Hollywood's hottest celebrities had just casually ambled into homeroom. Two soon-to-be baking stars sat amongst them, no longer mere sixth-graders concerned about everyday worries like story problems or science projects.

After an awkward moment, their classmates swarmed Jack's and Jillian's desks, giving them high fives and fist bumps.

Frieda Johnston asked Jack for an autograph.

"For my little sister," she said.

The clique of popular girls who had never uttered a word to Jillian shoved phones in her face and took selfies with her. They did the same with Jack, who stuck out his tongue and held up a victory sign for the cameras. One of them was Amy Eppington.

Crush back on! Jack thought. *Best . . . day . . . of . . . my . . . life!*

Jillian revived her wish to be a seventeen-year cicada. Deep underground.

Chad stood by Jack's desk. Flecks of blue and gold glitter dotted his red hair.

"Yeah, I was the guy behind the camera," he said, as if accepting an Academy Award. "I'd like to thank my family for their support, all my friends in the Sieberling Audiovisual Club, the guy at the electronics outlet who helped me pick out . . ."

Everyone returned to their desks when Ms. Riedel appeared in front of the class.

"Well, this is certainly an exciting day, isn't it?" she said, looking at Jillian and Jack. "I am so proud to have two of my students representing Sieberling School in the baking contest. Congratulations!"

Jack stood and bowed. Jillian sheepishly raised her right hand and gave a slight wave.

"Now open your grammar books. Today we're going to learn the difference between a colon and a semicolon."

That's it? Jack thought. *A few selfies, a round of congratulations, and, boom, we move on to punctuation?*

Ms. Riedel drew a colon and a semicolon on the blackboard.

"These two little marks may look similar, but don't be fooled."

Jack refused to open his textbook. He expected much more—a parade, fireworks, or Zombie Brunch coming out of retirement to greet him at the school's entrance. Instead, he got a grammar lesson.

Ms. Riedel noticed the closed book on Jack's desk and his defiant expression.

"Jack, life isn't going to stop because you'll be part of the Bakerstown Bonanza. We've got work to do. The lesson begins on page thirty-eight."

"But . . ."

"Page thirty-eight."

At lunch, Jack plopped his tray in front of Jillian. She sat in her usual spot in the back right corner of the cafeteria under the *A Good Book Can Take You Anywhere* poster, where she quietly read. This time, however, she wasn't alone. A group of fourth-graders milled about asking for autographs.

"Will you please sign my corn chip?" one asked.

Jillian took out a black marker and wrote her initials in the center of the nacho-flavored snack. She carved what faintly resembled a J and M, which was hard to do with cheese dust covering the tip of the marker.

"Thank you," he gushed. "This is going to be worth a lot of money."

"Strange day, huh?" Jack asked.

"From now on I'm charging for autographs," Jillian replied. "One dollar for a chip, two for a banana, three for a pint of chocolate milk, and five for a bologna sandwich."

"I'll pass that on to Bruce. Do you sign bags of dried crickets, too?"

"Yes, but that'll cost you a Hamilton."

Jack laughed. Of all the students at Sieberling School, he concluded that Jillian was the perfect baking companion, noting that she had a good sense of humor and wasn't afraid to take some risks in the kitchen. He seized the moment to learn more about his partner.

"Well, looks like we're teammates," he said.

"Yep," she replied, putting down her book.

"Chad and I had a big celebration last night when Farnsworth read my name."

"I bet it involved glitter. There's still some in your eyebrows."

"Who'd you watch with?"

"Grandma Rita."

"I saw you making rugelach with her in the video. Is she a big fan of Farnsworth like you?" Jack assumed that anyone who enjoyed baking worshipped his favorite tycoon.

Jillian hesitated before she answered. It would be simple to tell another lie and make things easier with Jack. Instead, the truth spilled out.

"No, she doesn't like him and neither do I."

"Yeah, he's the greatest . . . Wait, what did you say?"

"I said I can't stand him. He's a bully—and he's mean. Besides, he doesn't know the first thing about baking. I can tell."

Jack reeled back as if Jillian had struck him squarely on the forehead with one of Farnsworth's designer skillets. To him, saying Phineas Farnsworth III didn't know anything about baking was like accusing Einstein of not being able to solve one of Ms. Riedel's story problems.

I was wrong! I wouldn't have chosen Jillian at all!

"Farnsworth isn't mean. He has high standards. And look at what he's done for Ardmore. His family name is on half the buildings in this city. My dream is to be as famous as him someday. No, even more famous. My own pastry shops, my own cookware, my own TV show, my own—everything!"

Jillian remembered her mother's words: *If you don't have a dream to keep you going, you're just sleepwalking through life.* She listened as Jack rambled on about his dream of having his name and face plastered everywhere. To her, it sounded more like a nightmare.

"Okay, if you don't like Farnsworth, you must have a favorite chef at least?" Jack continued. "I bet it's Gregory Pritchard—he won the Bonanza in 1996 with his Five-Flavor O' Fudge Mountain. Oh, it's probably Melanie Etheridge. After her Razzle Dazzle Raspberry Triple Decker Flan won in 1964, so many people wanted to make it that there was a nationwide shortage of raspberries."

Jillian looked straight at Jack. "I don't know any of them. I never heard of Farnsworth or the Bonanza until I moved here."

Jack gave Jillian another hit-on-the-forehead-with-a-skillet look.

"Then why did you apply? What's your dream?"

This was what Jillian feared most about being in the spotlight. Questions she didn't want to answer. The fact was, Jillian did have a dream—an impossible one. She wanted her mother back.

"That's my business, not yours."

"Fine. Whether it's my business or not, we're going to need to practice. I'm not allowed to have people over to bake at my place after the whole cricket thing. Can I come to your house tonight? We need to get started right away."

"Sure, whatever."

As Jack got up to leave, a fifth-grader asked Jillian to autograph her granola bar wrapper. Her head throbbed.

Looking around the cafeteria, Jillian saw that every eye was focused on her. Soon, the entire town would be following her every move.

After lunch, Principal Dobkins called Jack and Jillian into his office. Jillian wondered if he had somehow found out she lied on her application. Jack thought he might be presenting him with his own personal key to the teachers' lounge on the second floor.

"First, I want to congratulate you both," Principal Dobkins said. "I understand the organizers received scores of applications from Sieberling."

"Thank you," Jack and Jillian said together.

"That being said, you each have an enormous responsibility. You will be representing not only the entire school but also all of Ardmore. There will be media from across the country attending and recording the event. It's of the *utmost* importance that you conduct yourselves in an appropriate manner."

What is he getting at? Jillian thought.

"Give me your personal assurance that you won't be putting anything *odd*—anything with six legs—in whatever you bake. Your science project has been the talk of the school for weeks."

Jack nodded. "No, we promise. No cricket cookies or katydid croissants. In fact, no winning recipe has ever included an insect or spider, so ours won't, either."

Principal Dobkins looked relieved.

"Well, good then. We're all counting on you to do your best. The Culinary Education Center would mean a great deal to Sieberling School. And it would be nice for our school to beat Old Harbor Academy and Feldspar Math and Science Institute at *something*. It's getting old finishing in third place in the Academic Challenge, Field Day, and the Annual Inventors' Fair. But just do your best. No pressure."

Walking back to class, Jillian gave Jack a troubled glance.

"I guess this isn't just about us," she said.

"Don't worry. We've got this."

Jillian wasn't so sure. She pulled the nacho-cheese-stained black marker from her pocket and looked at its ruined tip.

Well, that settles it. I'll be charging three dollars to autograph a corn chip, she thought. *Definitely three dollars.*

Chapter 16

Jack arrived at Grandma Rita's house carrying his Farnsworth Deluxe 5000 Food Processor, a tote bag brimming with gadgets, and his baking scrapbook. He had convinced himself that if Grandma Rita didn't like Phineas Farnsworth III, he was sure he wasn't going to like *her*.

Standing in the small kitchen, Jack noticed the outdated oven and a gas range with only two working burners. Aloe and jade plants crowded the windowsill. A photograph of a young woman holding a baby hung over the spice rack. Dented frying pans dangled on hooks above the sink. A wooden spoon, rolling pin, and sifter lay on the white laminate countertop.

This is where the chocolate rugelach was made? Jack thought. *Impossible!*

"This is my Grandma Rita," Jillian said.

"Pleased to meet you, Jack."

"It's nice to meet you, too." Jack wanted to ask her about Farnsworth right away. How could someone who had made such wonderful rugelach possibly dislike Ardmore's greatest contribution to the pastry world? It didn't make sense. But as a guest in her house, he didn't want to cause trouble.

"I liked the video you made," he continued.

"I enjoyed yours as well. I happen to be a big Zombie Brunch fan. I saw them in concert back in 1977. My ears are still ringing from the encore, 'Gluttony Buffet.'"

Jack stood slack-jawed. No one in his school knew anything about Zombie Brunch. He could find little about them on the Internet—one album, a brief tour, and a quiet breakup. The band members went their separate ways, fading into musical obscurity. Now here stood Jillian's bubbe—a pink streak splashed across her graying hair— talking about the only music that mattered in his life.

"I bought their album *Enjoy the Feast* at an oddity shop," he said. "It's what I play when I bake."

"What's your favorite track?" Grandma Rita asked. "Mine is the last one on the first side—'Hunger Road.'"

"Does it go 'yeah, yeah, yeah, yeah, yeah, yeah, yeah'?"

"That's the one!"

They all go yeah, yeah, yeah, yeah, yeah, yeah, yeah, Jillian thought.

The two talked for several minutes about the band. It

102

amazed Jillian how Grandma Rita could find common bonds with anybody and make strangers feel like old friends.

"Enough about Zombie Brunch. I'll be in the living room so you can get baking," Grandma Rita said.

"Please stay," Jack suggested. "You'll be able to give us some pointers."

Jillian frowned. She didn't want Jack to discover Grandma Rita's lack of skills in the kitchen.

"Oh, you both need to learn to work together," Grandma Rita said. "I should probably leave."

"You wouldn't be in the way," Jack said. "Is it okay with you, Jillian?"

"I guess so. We'll do the baking and you can watch. I thought we'd start with something easy."

Opening her mother's recipe book, Jillian turned to the page with a heading that read, *Oooh La La Lemon Bars*.

"They're basic but delicious," she said. "White powdered sugar on top, flaky crust, and a mix of sweet and tart."

Jack flipped through his scrapbook and found the page marked *Lemon*.

"This scrapbook is top secret," he said. "If it ever fell into the hands of the other contestants, we'd be doomed. You have to promise me you won't mention it to anyone."

Jillian rolled her eyes.

"I'm serious. You have to promise."

"Okay, I promise."

"Good. I've analyzed all seventy-four *Farnsworth Best of the Bonanza* cookbooks and watched every video of the previous competitions. Lemon is a mistake."

"Why?" Grandma Rita asked, peeking over Jack's shoulder.

"Only one winning baker has made a lemon dessert. I've watched Farnsworth's face when tasting anything with lemon. It's not pretty."

Jillian scanned Jack's notes. *Farnsworth is always sour when it comes to lemon. Avoid at all costs! When using fruit fillings, strawberry or peach are better choices.*

Jack pointed to a chart. "It's a pie chart, get it? Peach pastries have won seven percent of the time. Lemon ranks at the bottom. Blackberry and strawberry are tied at eleven percent."

Jillian remained unimpressed. "I don't care what your *pie* chart says. Everyone loves these lemon bars."

"Farnsworth won't," Jack said with urgency. "Besides, lemon bars are too small. We'll have to impress him with something big—that's what usually wins. A little cookie isn't going to do it."

"Why don't you make the lemon bars anyway?" Grandma Rita said. "Right now you're just practicing together. You don't have to make them for the contest."

"Good point," Jack said. "I have some huge ideas for what we'll actually bake. It's all right here in my scrapbook."

Jillian looked at her mother's recipe book. "I have some ideas, too," she said tersely. *And I'm not going to let you boss me around, Jack Fineman*, she thought. *We need to win this . . . and you can't do it without me.*

"I suggest you get started," Grandma Rita urged. "You can decide on the contest recipe later."

"Good idea," Jack said. "We'll pretend we're at the Bonanza. Ready? Let's go."

Jack and Jillian soon forgot all about whether Farnsworth preferred gooseberries or blackberries as they went to work. Jack had imagined them maneuvering around the small kitchen in a well-choreographed ballet of blending, whisking, pouring, and baking. Instead, they bumped into each other scrambling for a bag of flour. Somehow, a yellow waterfall of lemon juice cascaded off the counter. They grabbed for a bottle of vanilla extract at the same time, sending it crashing to the floor. Their first baking session as Sieberling School's team had quickly turned into a discordant clash of Zombie Brunch versus Vivaldi, both blasting simultaneously at full volume.

They looked at each other puzzled, unsure of how baking the cricket cookies had come so easily but making the lemon bars was becoming such a challenge.

"Maybe you're nervous," Grandma Rita said. "Try to relax and work together."

"I knew that lemon bars were a mistake," Jack said, pointing to his scrapbook.

Jillian ignored him. When each ingredient was added to the mixing bowl, she closed her eyes and breathed deeply.

"What are you doing?" Jack asked.

"Adding a special ingredient," Jillian said.

"O . . . kay," Jack said. "And what is that?"

"Oh, never mind."

Once baked, Jillian pulled the pan out of the oven and began cutting the sheet into squares.

"Make them perfectly even," Jack said. "Presentation matters."

If that's what it takes to win—fine! Jillian thought.

Jack poured powdered sugar into the sifter and handed it to Grandma Rita.

"Why don't you finish them?" he said.

Bad idea! Jillian thought. *Using a sifter can be tricky. All it takes is a few light taps on the side. Otherwise it's a mess.*

"I'd be honored," Grandma Rita said. She jiggled the metal sifter so vigorously that the dessert became buried under an avalanche of white.

Jack watched in disbelief. In that instant he realized Jillian did not learn to bake from her grandmother. And he knew their baking session had been a complete failure. He saw his dreams of pastry supremacy rapidly slipping away.

"Look at these! Ruined!" Jack said. "By the way, great

job with that vanilla extract. Farnsworth would be very impressed."

Jillian didn't back down. "You're the one who knocked over the lemon juice," she snapped. "And that Farnsworth food processor you brought over is a noisy piece of junk!"

"No, it's not. It puts out 720 watts of power, comes with intuitive speed and dicing controls, and is fortified with anti-slip feet."

"What does that even mean?" Jillian threw her hands up.

"It means it's really awesome," Jack said, searching his brain for another comeback. "And what's with this secret ingredient you're magically putting into the recipe? All it does is slow us down."

"You'd never understand."

"And . . . and . . . you said you learned to bake from your grandmother! That's a lie."

Jillian froze as the room went silent, save for the *drip, drip, drip* of lemon juice falling like tears onto the linoleum floor. She covered her face.

"What did I say?" Jack asked.

"I guess it's pretty obvious that I'm not the great baking instructor here," Grandma Rita said, brushing sugar off her sleeves. "Tell him the truth, Jillian. He's your teammate. I'll leave you two alone."

It took Jillian all her courage to tell Jack the real reason she had applied to be in the Bakerstown Bonanza. But before she did, she had Jack make a promise.

"What I'm going to tell you is personal. This is between you and me. No one else."

"Not even Chad?"

"No one, including Farnsworth. I didn't put any of this in my application, so he doesn't know about it. I don't want to talk about any of this during the Bonanza. You swear?"

"Yes, I swear. You can count on me."

"Okay, here goes," Jillian said, taking a deep breath. "I learned everything I know about baking from my mother. Our family owned a pastry shop in Seattle. That's where I lived before we moved to Ardmore. My mom and I baked everything together. But the shop closed and we had to sell all the equipment. We owed the bank so much money that my father and I had to move in with Grandma Rita. That's why I need to win the Bonanza—to help out my dad."

Jack nodded. He had many friends whose parents were divorced. He assumed this was the case with Jillian, too.

"Did your mother stay in Seattle? Do you get to visit her?" Jack asked. "That must be tough."

"No, Jack, they're not divorced," Jillian said, casting her eyes down at her sneakers. "My mother died. I'll never see her again. I don't talk about it because it's . . . well, it's just too hard right now. And it's private. That's why I made up the story about Grandma Rita to get in the contest."

Jack listened in silence as Jillian talked further about

her mother, Joan of Hearts, and the wooden spoon with a chip like a missing tooth. He had never faced such hardships. His life revolved around baking, goofing off with Chad, staying out of Bruce's way, and plotting his future.

"I'm sorry," he said. "You must have been sad."

"Still am. Not *always* anymore, but a lot of the time."

Jack tried to comprehend what to him was incomprehensible.

"This was my mother's recipe book," Jillian said, flipping through it so Jack could see the messages framing each page. She stopped where it read *Chocolate Rugelach.*

"So you made the rugelach without any help?" Jack asked.

"No, I didn't do it alone. Grandma Rita told me jokes while I baked. And my mother *was* with me—right here." Jillian put her hand over her heart. "But I thought you hated my rugelach. I saw that awful face you made when you tasted it."

Now it was Jack's turn to tell the truth.

"I made that face because I was jealous. Your rugelach was the best thing I had ever eaten. *Ever.*"

Jack could barely believe his own words. For the first time in his life, he had admitted that he was only second best. At least *this* time.

Shocked by Jack's announcement, Jillian said, "Thanks. That would have meant a lot to my mother, knowing that you enjoyed it so much. That's why she baked."

"So, be honest. Did you like my butterscotch basil brownies?"

"They were good. No, very good," Jillian said slowly. "But something was missing, like you forgot an ingredient."

"Left out an ingredient? No way. Not possible."

"Like I said, they were *very* good."

But not as good as your rugelach.

After Jack left, Jillian sat alone in the kitchen and sampled one of the lemon bars.

Surprisingly decent, she thought. *There's love in there for sure—I can taste it. Of course, my fight with Jack came after we baked. Then they wouldn't have tasted like much at all. But they're not nearly tart enough for me. We'll have to do better if we're going to win. Much better.*

Jillian's thoughts were interrupted by the rumble of a Chevy Cavalier pulling into the driveway and the realization that, in a few moments, she would have to confront another one of her lies.

Dad! What am I going to tell him about the Bonanza? He doesn't even know I entered! Argh! What a day!

When Mr. Mermelstein entered the house, Jillian shoved a copy of that day's *Ardmore Star* in the kitchen junk drawer. She hoped her father hadn't already seen the front-page headline: *Farnsworth III Selects Six Ardmore Students for Bonanza.*

He needs to hear it first from me, she thought.

"Hi, Jills," he said. "How was your day? It was the same old, same old for me. Nothing new on the road crew."

He hasn't read it!

"Well, I have something important . . ."

"Hey, do I smell lemon bars?" he asked, taking off his winter coat. He scanned the cluttered countertop. "Looks like you've been busy in the kitchen."

"Yes, we have. Please try one," she said. "We made them just before you came home."

"*We?* Oh, don't tell me Grandma Rita helped. That would explain the powdered sugar. Kind of like what Mother Nature did to me," he said, shaking snow off his coat before hanging it up.

Jillian faked a laugh. She had something big to tell, and it was no easier than revealing to Jack the truth about her mother.

"Grandma did the sifting, but there was someone else here baking. Jack Fineman."

"He's the boy you baked cricket cookies with. That's wonderful! Nice to see you're finally making some friends here."

"Uh, Dad . . ."

He took a bite of a lemon bar.

"Fabulous," he said. "Looks like you and Jack—and Grandma Rita—make a pretty good team."

"Okay, here goes," she said—for the second time that day. "Actually, we *are* a team. Jack is my partner in the Bakerstown Bonanza. We're going to represent Sieberling School. Isn't that great?"

Jillian could tell from her father's expression that, maybe, he didn't agree.

"Jills, why didn't you tell me about this?" he said.

"You're so busy all the time. And I didn't think you would let me enter."

"You're right about that. I read about the Bonanza in the paper a couple of weeks ago. It's a very big deal. There will be news coverage from all the major networks. And thousands of phones pointed at you. I know how these contests work. They ask questions about your personal business, peek into your living room windows, dig into your family history, and make a spectacle of your life for everyone to see. This is a hard time for us. I'm not comfortable sharing our past—and our money troubles— with the rest of the world."

"But Dad . . ."

"And, by the way, I don't remember signing any permission form for you to enter."

"I told you it was for a school field trip. I'm sorry. I didn't think there was a chance they'd pick me. Really, I don't even want to be in it."

"Then why did you apply?" It was Jack's exact question from that morning.

"The winners split $150,000. I thought we could use the money."

"Oh, Jillian," her father said, hugging her. "You didn't have to."

"I wanted to help. And I was careful about what I wrote on the application. I didn't mention Mom, or the bakery, or you, or what I'd do with the money. I promise. It didn't feel right."

"What did you tell them?"

"That every time my Grandma Rita bakes, I learn something new."

"Like what *not* to do?"

"Exactly."

At breakfast the next morning, Jillian made a confession to Grandma Rita.

"I don't know how I am going to work with Jack. He's a miniature version of Phineas Farnsworth III—with a lot more hair. And you know how I feel about *him*."

"Give it time," Grandma Rita said. "You don't know much about Jack. Come to think of it, we don't know much about Farnsworth, either."

"I don't want to know anything about him!"

"Maybe you should. It might help your chances of winning. Why don't you google him and see what you find?"

Jillian typed in *Phineas Farnsworth III* and hit Enter.

Pages and pages of references appeared on the screen. They scrolled through entries detailing the history of the Farnsworth Baking Supply Company, its line of ingredients and equipment, interviews, and photos. She wrote down key points from what she found:

- At the age of twenty-seven, Farnsworth III was appointed CEO of the family business in 1979 after his father passed away in a yachting accident.
- The first baking gadget he created—the SureFire SiftMaster—became an overnight hit. Millions were sold worldwide.
- The huge demand for Farnsworth products forced the company to triple the size of its factory in Ardmore. Construction was completed in 1980, with much of the factory's expansions occurring on Market and Maple streets.
- He has been judging the Bakerstown Bonanza for forty years.

"This is pointless," Jillian sighed. "Every website repeats the same information. Jack has already told me some of this."

"Wait, look here," Grandma Rita said, pointing at the screen. "Now we're getting somewhere."

Buried on the last page was an article from *The Kensington Weekly*, the student newspaper of Kensington

College in central Ohio. A photo of a much younger Phineas Farnsworth III was below a headline that read, *Meet the Heir to the Farnsworth Baking Throne.*

Jillian printed out the interview.

Q: I understand that many famous people visited the Farnsworth family estate, such as presidents and the Queen of England. What is your fondest memory of growing up there?

A: *My fondest memory? It was a plate of home-baked chocolate brownies. I recall devouring every one. I believe I was ten at the time. To be honest, I have never tasted anything as good since.*

Q: Did your mother and father do a lot of baking around the house?

A: *Actually, no. When you're running an international business, there's little time for such domestic pursuits. The brownies were made by my nanny—Miss Alexandra. She called me her "Little Cupcake." She'd tell me the funniest stories. And we'd go to the park every Thursday afternoon. There were picnics in the summer and ice skating on a pond in our backyard. Just the two of us. She was always there for me, even when my parents weren't.*

Q: What happened to her? Are you still in touch?

A: *I'm afraid not. It was so sudden. So unexpected. So very sad . . .*

Q: Could you explain?

A: *Well . . . I don't think that's any of your business, now, is it? Another personal question like that and this interview is officially over. I thought you were supposed to ask me about trends in food manufacturing!*

Jillian folded the paper and placed it in the back of her mother's recipe book.

My little cupcake? I bet no one calls him that now! she thought.

ℭhapter 17

ack couldn't get Jillian's story out of his head. Now he understood why she had sat so quietly all these months in the back of the classroom. He knew why she had entered the Bakerstown Bonanza even though she couldn't stand the sight of Phineas Farnsworth III. Also, for the first time in his life, he had met someone who knew as much about food as himself. He finally had someone to discuss the best way to cream butter or separate eggs.

But one thought pushed all others aside: *Jillian's mother is gone, forever.*

Jack knocked on the door of his mother's study, where she often reviewed medical records after a long day at Ardmore General Hospital.

"Mom, can we talk?"

"Certainly. How's my local celebrity?"

"Fine. Jillian and I made lemon bars. The execution

was a little bit of a disaster, but they turned out fine. I saved you some."

"Lemon is my favorite. You didn't put anything *unusual* in them, I hope."

"Maybe a bit too much powdered sugar on top, but no crickets." Jack hesitated. "Can I ask you a question?"

"Shoot."

"How did I end up in this family? Bruce lives on bologna sandwiches. You and Dad have no interest in baking. Did you bring home the wrong baby from the hospital? Am I adopted?"

"So many questions! First off, you're a Fineman through and through. As I've said before, we brought home the right baby. And for the hundredth time, you were *not* adopted."

"Then why am I such a foodie?"

"You are just like my grandmother—Bubbe Leah. She loved everything about food. She spent all her time in the small bakery she and Zayde Stan owned at the corner of Market and Maple streets here in town. It broke her heart when it was torn down—brick by brick—and replaced with another business." Mrs. Fineman spat out the words "another business" as if she had tasted spoiled milk. She lightly pounded on her desk each time she said "brick."

"Your grandparents owned a bakery? Why didn't you mention this before?"

"It's not an easy story to tell."

"Why?"

"Because baking was all they knew. All they ever did. Zayde Stan handled the financial end of the business while Bubbe Leah made challah for Friday night dinners, hamantaschen for Purim, macaroons for Passover, and sufganiyot for Hanukkah. Oh, how she loved to see her customers enjoying what she made! People came from all over to buy her cherry-covered cheesecakes. Her specialty, though, was rugelach."

"Rugelach? What flavor?"

"Chocolate."

"You're kidding, right?"

"Why would I kid about that? I can still taste her chocolate rugelach to this day. Even though the memory is a little bitter."

"How come?" Jack asked. He couldn't imagine how anything about baking could be bitter at all.

"Because baking took Bubbe Leah away from the family. Every morning, year after year after year, she rose before dawn to walk to the shop. Long before anyone in the city ate their breakfast, she hauled sacks of flour, poured batter out of mixers, kneaded dough, bent in front of hot ovens, and moved heavy cooling trays. We rarely saw her, rarely had a family breakfast. She worked every day, except on the Sabbath."

Jack thought about his mornings. He usually hit the Snooze button on his alarm clock four or five times before his father pounded on his bedroom door.

"It's a good thing my bubbe was a hefty woman. A strong woman," Mrs. Fineman said. "Otherwise, she wouldn't have lasted a week. Grab the photo book, will you?"

Jack took the album off its shelf and handed it to his mother. She flipped through until she pulled out a photograph of a large woman wearing an apron and hairnet. A thin man in a suit and holding a hat stood beside her. The sign above the door of the business read: *Goldfarb Bakery. Est. 1944.* The inscription on the back read, *Leah and Stanley Goldfarb, 1980.* Jack peered closely at Bubbe Leah's face. Her expression showed neither happiness nor sorrow. To Jack, it looked as if his great-grandmother had given up.

"This was taken the last day at the bakery—only a few hours before it was torn down. In your hands is a woman who toiled her entire life to make food for others only to have her business taken away in the name of the public good."

Jack noticed Bubbe Leah's scarred hands, marred by too many nicks from a sharp bread knife.

"No matter how hard she worked, I don't remember her ever frowning—until the bakery was gone," Mrs. Fineman said, pausing several seconds to compose herself. "Zayde Stan believed that when the building was demolished, a big part of her died that day."

Mrs. Fineman wiped away a tear.

"At her funeral a few years later, my mother told me, 'I don't want my daughter spending her days covered in flour at four in the morning.' Remember, Jack, some dreams come with a price. It's not all about bright lights and baking contests."

"Can I keep the photo, Mom?"

"Yes, but take good care of it."

In his room, Jack placed the photograph in the back of his scrapbook. He closed it, finally certain that he was, indeed, in the right family.

Chapter 18

The Bonanza was drawing closer. Jack and Jillian practiced making pastries from Jillian's recipe book, along with desserts of Jack's own creation.

Chad joined them to offer words of encouragement. Despite his efforts, Jillian and Jack argued at least three times per baking session. And they still hadn't decided on what to bake for the contest.

After some thought, Jack rejected Jillian's suggestion to make her mother's chocolate rugelach recipe.

"Yes, it's incredible, but not impressive enough. We need something epic. Something extraordinary. That's what Farnsworth likes for his cookbook covers."

Jack insisted on a four-tiered cake, each layer with a different flavor—maple, banana, coconut, and vanilla.

"I've studied seventy-four years of winning recipes," he said. "These are the top four flavors bakers have used. If we put them together in a single cake—boom!—we can't lose."

Jillian crossed her arms.

"I see your point, but it sounds like a train wreck to me. It's too much. How about we make almond cookies?"

Jillian read aloud the notes in the margin of her mother's Chewy Raspberry Almond Cookie recipe: *"Almonds—a symbol of early blooming, of better days. Always start the week with an almond recipe."* She paused. "The contest is on a Sunday—the start of the week. Almond cookies would be perfect."

"Not to Farnsworth," Jack said. "According to my scrapbook, a recipe with almond flavor has only won once, way back in 1952."

"At least they won't be a train wreck."

"Who says?"

Chad couldn't take their bickering any longer.

"Hey, I've got an idea. Mom coordinates team-building activities where she works. I think you guys need some serious team-building."

"Explain," Jack said, clutching a bag of almonds.

"Instead of being in the office all the time, she and her coworkers go out and do a fun activity together, like hiking on nature trails or playing volleyball at the community center."

"And the point is?" Jillian asked, wrestling the almonds away from Jack.

"It gives everyone a chance to get to know each other outside of work. It could help you win by building commas and radii."

"I think you mean camaraderie," Jack said, grabbing the bag back.

"No, I'm pretty sure Mom says it builds commas and radii, though I have no idea what hiking or volleyball has to do with punctuation and math."

Jack shook his head, knowing that Chad wasn't joking.

Chad met Jack and Jillian at the Ardmore Indoor Amusement Park. The sprawling complex had thirty bowling lanes, a rock climbing wall, ball pits, a trampoline, basketball courts, a Ferris wheel, an arcade, an eighteen-hole miniature golf course, a candy shop, and a restored merry-go-round.

The three started by slipping into harnesses for the rock climbing wall. Jack knew Chad was much better at snowboarding down a real mountain than climbing up a fake one indoors. Jack and Jillian scrambled to the top at the same time. On the way down, Jack's sneaker snagged on one of the holds, allowing Jillian to zip by and touch bottom before he could untangle himself.

"Let's do that again!" she said, grinning.

"No, let's go bowling," Jack demanded.

Jack easily won, racking up spares and strikes. As he hurled the ten-pound bowling ball down the lane, the sound of Zombie Brunch songs pounded in his head. Jillian and Chad struggled to keep their balls out of the gutter. The final scores: Jack, 128, Chad, 88, and Jillian, 73.

"Up for another game, anyone?" Jack asked as he slurped a lime slushy.

"No," Jillian said. "Let's try out the trampoline."

"Trampoline, huh? You're on!"

Chad sensed tension rising between his friends. Why was everything a competition between them?

"Let's do something as a team," he suggested as Jack and Jillian raced away.

On the trampoline, Jillian bounded higher than Jack by a foot. In basketball, Jack made more free throws. Playing Whack-A-Marmot, Jillian outdid Jack by three points. Chad watched helplessly as an entire community of mechanical rodents was depopulated without Jack or Jillian speaking a word to each other.

"How about I beat you at miniature golf?" Jillian asked.

"How about we go home?" Chad pleaded.

Jack lined up his golf ball at the first hole—a straight shot into an elephant's trunk, out its tail, and into the metal cup in the left corner of the felt-topped green.

As he was about to putt, Jack heard his name called. He turned around and stared directly into a shimmering sea of orange-and-teal fabric. It was Bruce.

"So this is how Chef Boyar-Geek gets ready to be

humiliated in front of the entire town," Bruce said. "Step aside. You're in my domain now—the House of Bruce. A place where your baking skills mean zip. Watch me dazzle you with the finer points of golf."

The finer points of golf? Jack thought. *It's an elephant's trunk for crying out loud!*

Jillian approached Bruce with her putter in one hand and a pink dimpled ball in the other.

"So you think you can beat us?" she asked.

No!!! Jack's brain screamed. *Don't challenge him! Bruce is amazing at golf! It's all he does!*

"Of course I can." Bruce laughed, hitching up his pants. "Wanna bet?"

Bet? What are you talking about? Jack thought.

"Sure! If I beat all three of you—which I could do blindfolded—Jack has to tell the whole world during the Bone-an-za, 'My dear brother, Bruce, is my hero, my one-and-only inspiration. And he rocks at golf.'"

Jack tried to interrupt, but Jillian couldn't be stopped.

"Okay. And if we win you have to go on camera and announce that Jack makes the best . . . oatmeal . . . cookies . . . in . . . the . . . universe."

"Chirp, chirp," Chad said.

Bruce swooned at the thought of brushing his teeth after gorging on the cookies.

"*And* you have to ride the merry-go-round on an animal of our choice," Chad said.

Caught up in Chad's enthusiasm, Jack added, "Holding one of those big swirly lollipops from the candy shop!"

"Fair enough," Bruce sneered. "Eighteen holes—lowest score wins." He knew about Jack's embarrassing attempts at golf. He suspected Chad was no expert, either. As for Jillian, he felt confident no girl could ever beat him.

Bruce went first. He eyed his target before pulling back the putter with precision. He tapped his yellow ball directly into the pachyderm's trunk. Seconds later it popped out its tail, bounced twice, and went directly into the bottom of the hole.

"Say it, Jack! 'Bruce is my heeerrrooo!'" his brother said, dancing the jig he had hoped to perform weeks ago.

"Not so fast," Jack said. "Watch this!"

He swung wildly, sending his putter airborne. It bounded off the elephant's left ear and landed near a Whack-A-Marmot console. Chad's putt was no better, but at least he held on to the club. His ball hit the plastic divider between the animal's nostrils and rolled back to its original spot at his feet.

Bruce mocked them by clapping slowly.

"Bravo, boys! Are you sure you don't want to quit now before this gets ugly?" he said.

"I was going to ask you the same thing," Jillian said.

She walked coolly to the plastic pad and set her ball down. She gripped the putter, winked at Bruce, and struck the ball with the same confidence she frosted a molasses cookie or iced a German chocolate cupcake. The pink sphere went smoothly into the trunk, out the tail, and in the cup. She calmly retrieved it and strode to the next hole.

Jack let out a cheer. Chad threw up his arms, wishing he had brought his air horn and a bag of glitter. Seventeen holes later, Bruce wished he had never met Jillian Mermelstein, the girl who knew how to swing a mean putter.

Jack, Jillian, and Chad watched Bruce sitting astride an ostrich on the merry-go-round holding a red-green-and-yellow sucker about the size of a dinner plate.

"You were awesome, Jillian," Jack said. "Where did you learn . . ."

"Grandma Rita is great at golf, too."

Chad beamed. "You two have definitely built a whole bunch of commas and radii today."

"Yes, we'll make a good team," Jack said.

"We'll see," Jillian said. "First, there's something else you need to hear."

Chapter 19

Back in Grandma Rita's kitchen, Jack's brain buzzed with the image of Jillian sinking a perfect putt on the eighteenth hole. She had banked it off the right-side rail, sending the ball through a loop the loop, into a tunnel, and down a twisting ramp. It straddled the lip of the cup before hitting the bottom with a satisfying *plunk*. Bruce's ball had circled the hole three times before resting an inch away.

Jack had watched Jillian closely on every hole. Earlier she had smashed marmots like a professional exterminator and scaled the rock wall with the nimbleness of a mountain goat. There was no doubt in Jack's mind: Jillian could handle the pressure of competing against the contestants from Old Harbor and Feldspar without breaking a sweat.

Jillian emerged from her bedroom holding her mother's recipe book. It was open to the first page.

"Read this out loud," she said.

"*Cooking is not a contest,*" Jack read. "*It is a prayer whispered humbly as the sun rises. When no one else is looking. When the rest of the world sleeps.*"

"I want you to memorize this."

"Why? The Bakerstown Bonanza *is* a contest. It always has been."

"Please! If you're my teammate, you have to know this."

"I don't see how it's going to help, but if I must . . ."

Jack wrote down the words in his scrapbook.

Then Jillian turned to a page with the heading, *The King's Most Extraordinary Forever More Cake.*

"A cake! That should be excellent practice. Does it have four layers, each with a different flavor?" Jack asked, hopefully.

"No, it's not a recipe. It was my mother's favorite fairy tale. She used to read it to me. Now I'm going to read it to you."

Jack scoffed. "I'm too old for fairy tales. Can we make a cake instead?"

"This is important, Jack. I need you to listen carefully."

"Okay, I owe you big-time. I got to see my brother riding an ostrich today. Read away."

Jillian began.

Long ago in olden times, a king ruled a land known as Forever More. It was called Forever More because the good people of the kingdom were forevermore miserable. That's because the king was forevermore unhappy with everything, so he took out his frustrations on whomever and whatever crossed his path.

Every morning, the king screamed at the sun for being too bright and too yellow. He yelled at the royal cook when the eggs were the slightest bit runny. During his midday walk, he shouted at the ground beneath his feet for being excessively hard and accused the sky of lacking creativity.

"Blue! Blue! Blue! All I see today is blue!"

The king was most unreasonable at dinnertime. He banged his spoon on the table because the chicken soup was too soupy. He threw a tantrum claiming the silver forks clashed with the green peas. Dessert was either too sweet, or too bland, or "not even fit for the palace mice."

Terrified members of his court barely lasted a few days before being dismissed. When the king commanded that the royal baker plan his birthday cake, his assistant reminded him that he had just fired the baker for making a pineapple upside-down cake right-side up.

"That makes five bakers this month," the assistant said, ducking as the king flung a plate at his head.

So the king ordered the court crier to issue an urgent proclamation:

"Hear ye! Hear ye! His royal majesty requires all the bakers of Forever More to make a cake to celebrate his birthday. One, and only one, cake will be chosen for the

131

gala. The baker of this extraordinary cake will be rewarded with a chest of gold and rubies. All other cake-makers will be imprisoned in the dungeon. Present all cakes at the castle gate tomorrow at noon."

When the bakers of the kingdom heard the news, they panicked. None had a clue how to bake a cake that would please the king, for as far as anyone could remember, the king had never been pleased.

With their freedom at stake, the bakers used the best ingredients they could find. Cakes were topped with buttery icings and fresh-picked strawberries. Some mixed in the finest flour and milk from rare Turkish goats. Cakes with twelve, fifteen, and even eighteen layers towered toward the ceiling.

The king sat on his throne and waited impatiently, grumbling at the castle sundial for being so lazy.

At noon on the next day, a line of bakers stretched for a mile to the castle doors. Trembling, the bakers held cakes that would either unlock a chest of riches or condemn them to a life sentence in the dungeon.

One by one, they presented their cakes to the king. And one by one, each was led to the dungeon by the palace guards.

"Too salty," the king complained.

"This strawberry's shape troubles me."

"I am not in the mood for chocolate."

As the sky began to darken, only one baker remained—

an old man wearing tattered clothes and holding a simple one-layer cake with vanilla icing. The king looked at the old man and his cake with the utmost contempt.

"What is this?" the king snorted.

"Should I take him to the dungeon?" a guard barked.

"Please," the old man said. "I beg that you try it."

And the king did. After a long pause, he took a second bite and then a third before putting his fork down.

"I have found my birthday cake!" the king declared, smiling for the first time since he was a child. "Give this fine man the chest of gold and rubies!"

"Bless you. Bless you," the old man said, tears of relief streaking down his face.

"In exchange for your reward, I demand the recipe for this extraordinary cake so my royal baker can make it for me anytime I wish."

The king's assistant chimed in. "But all the bakers in Forever More are in your dungeon," he said, ducking as a fork whizzed over his head.

"Then I will make it myself and I will be forevermore happy."

The old man wrote out the recipe and gave it to the king. He took the chest of gold and rubies and rushed back to his home on the edge of the forest to share the glorious news with his wife and sons.

That night the king devoured the rest of the cake, but it did not completely satisfy his hunger. He pulled out the recipe and followed each direction exactly as written. Coming out of the oven, the cake smelled wonderful. But it tasted awful. He tried the recipe again and again and again with the same results. The more he baked, the angrier he became and the worse the cake tasted.

"Find the old man and bring him to me this instant!" the king howled.

The palace guards searched the kingdom. They found the old man and dragged him before the king.

"I have followed your recipe, but my cakes do not taste like yours," the king said, pointing to the fifteen cakes on the table, each with a single bite taken out of them. "Tell me what ingredient you have left out of the recipe. Your very life depends on it."

"I was afraid this would happen," the old man said.

"What do you mean?"

"It is not what I have left out. It is what you have left out—love."

"Love!" the king bellowed. His face was beet red with rage. "What folly is this?"

"When I make cakes, I think about the love I feel for my beautiful wife and sons. I pour that love into the batter. This is as important as the milk and sugar. That is why my cake tastes so extraordinary."

"Then you will be my royal baker who will make this cake anytime I desire."

"But, Your Majesty, it will not taste as you wish, I assure you."

Angered even further, the king threw the old man into the dungeon with the other bakers.

That night the king tossed and turned in his royal chambers. He could not get the old man's words out of his mind.

The next morning, the king summoned his guards.

"Release the bakers from the dungeon and send them home. Immediately."

"Yes, sire."

The king ran to the royal kitchen. He mixed flour, eggs, butter, and milk into a bowl. As he stirred, he closed his eyes and imagined the bakers returning to their families— the tears of joy, the warm embraces, and the sweet sound of laughter. Making the simple vanilla icing, he saw the old man hugging his sons and waltzing with his wife. From the top of his head to the bottom of his feet, he felt a warm glow that he had never experienced before.

When the cake came out of the oven, the king took a bite.

It was extraordinary.

Jillian put down the recipe book.

"It's a nice fairy tale," Jack said. "Thanks for reading it to me."

"But it's more than a fairy tale," Jillian insisted. "It's true."

"Which part?"

"All of it. When she baked, my mother always said: Don't forget to add the most important ingredient—love."

"Sorry, but I'm not buying it. Look in any of the Farnsworth cookbooks. Love is never mentioned. And if it's true, then why is Grandma Rita's baking so . . . uh . . ."

"Indescribable?"

"Yes. I'm sure she puts love in her baking."

"You still have to be a good baker. Adding love is the extra boost that makes something good . . . well . . . extraordinary."

"True or not, we *can't* talk about this! We'll get laughed off the stage. Guaranteed!"

That night Jillian's first chocolate rugelach lesson with her mother played again in her mind.

"Okay, Jills, we've rolled the dough. Do you know what's next?"

"Baking it in the oven?"

"Not quite. This is part of the recipe you won't find in any book."

"Where would you find it?"

Jillian's mother pointed to her heart. "Right here. As I bake, I pull memories from my memory box. Sometimes I'll remember my grandmother and the wonderful smells coming from her kitchen. I can see her singing 'Hinei Ma Tov' as she rolled dough for a crust. My memory box is so full I can always find something new to pull out. A good baker never enters the kitchen without a fully stocked memory box."

She showed Jillian how to lightly brush the rugelach with an egg wash. Then she gently sprinkled sugar on top before putting them in the oven.

"What were you thinking of this time, Mom?" Jillian asked.

"Usually these memories are kept inside. But since you asked, I was remembering the day you were born—the first time I rocked you in my arms and sang you a lullaby."

Jillian watched her mother glide around the kitchen like a winged angel carried along on a cloud of flour and granulated sugar. When Jillian took a bite of the chocolate rugelach, she filed the taste under the letter R in her own memory box.

ℭhapter 20

Two weeks later, the parents of the six contestants received a hand-delivered letter. Jillian, her father, and Grandma Rita sat down at the kitchen table and read it together.

Greetings!

On behalf of the Farnsworth Baking Supply Company, let me say we are delighted to have your child participating in the 75th Anniversary Edition of the Bakerstown Bonanza. Please read the following carefully as it contains important details regarding the event.

- All contestants and family members must attend a pre-contest briefing session at the Farnsworth family estate on Saturday, April 5. A limousine will pick you up at your home at 9 a.m.

- Participation is mandatory. Contracts will be signed at this time.
- On-camera interviews will be conducted. These will be projected onto video screens during the event. Wear clothing that reflects your personality.
- The Farnsworth Baking Supply Company reserves the right to use these interviews at our own discretion.

I'm looking forward to meeting all of you in person.

Best regards,

Liz Escobar, Bakerstown Bonanza Coordinator

Jillian noticed the word "discretion" again. She, her father, and Grandma Rita had rehearsed what they would say so their stories didn't conflict. They agreed not to mention Jillian's mother.

"Your mother would never have been part of something like this," Mr. Mermelstein said. "But now that we're involved in this thing, we will keep our private lives private."

Jack and his family watched as a gold limousine measuring thirty feet long stopped in front of their house. Once inside, Jack ran his hand over the vehicle's plush red velvet interior and poured himself a glass of grapefruit juice from a mini-fridge. He stretched out his legs and put his feet up on an empty seat.

"Still think baking is a waste of time?" he asked Bruce, who was fidgeting with a remote control trying to find the Golf Channel on the limo's television.

"Put your feet down, Jack!" Mrs. Fineman scolded. "And don't break anything! The last thing I want is to owe the Farnsworth family a nickel."

Jack tapped on the glass separating the Finemans from the uniformed chauffeur, who pressed a button to roll down the divider.

"Once around the park," Jack said in a voice imitating Farnsworth's deep growl. "Then we'll stop for a spot of ice cream, and then it's off to the spa for manicures."

Bruce searched the remote in his hand, hoping to find an Eject button to launch his little brother through the limo's open sunroof.

"It's official," Bruce said. "You are Ardmore's—no, the world's—biggest dweeb."

"I may be a dweeb," Jack said. "But remember it was me who was invited to the Farnsworth family estate. You're just excess baggage. Hand me the ice tongs. I need to freshen my drink."

Meanwhile, a black limousine carrying Jillian and her family snaked through Ardmore's brick streets, cruising past the Farnsworth factory and rows of single-family homes built for workers who flocked to the city as the company expanded. Mr. Mermelstein pointed out several potholes he had recently filled.

Miles from downtown, six limousines turned down a winding lane marked *Private*. Rows of sycamore trees framed the long driveway. The drivers ignored the *No Trespassing* signs and rolled forward to an iron gate, which swung open as if by magic. The caravan of young bakers arrived at a four-story, golden-domed mansion so large it looked as if it could swallow all their homes in a single gulp. The Farnsworth family crest was featured prominently on the iron-studded wooden entrance.

"I read that there are seven bathrooms on the first floor alone," Jack said.

"Why seven?" Mr. Fineman asked, looking up at the gargoyles leaning over the tiled roof.

"Duh, Dad. One for each day of the week."

"Of course! How silly of me."

The oak door creaked open to reveal a woman dressed in a white linen pantsuit and holding a clipboard.

"Hello, all. I'm Liz Escobar. Please call me Liz. Let me welcome you to the Farnsworth home. I take it your ride here was pleasant. We have a great deal to accomplish, so let's get started."

She led the group into the foyer and down the main hallway. Jack's eyes darted in every direction, making sure not to miss a single detail.

I can't believe I'm in Phineas Farnsworth's mansion! Jack thought.

As he walked, Jack recognized framed baking memorabilia hanging on the walls.

"That's Edna Harberg's apron from the first year," he shouted. "See! It still has the rhubarb stains on the left pocket. Amazing!"

"Keep it down, would you?" Bruce whispered. "People are staring."

"Oooooh! There's Lawrence Gregerson's purple chef's hat from 2003. I'd know it anywhere."

"Okay, Jack, calm down. Breathe!" Mr. Fineman urged.

"How can I? That's . . . that's . . . the rare *Farnsworth Best of the Bonanza* from 1983. The one with the typo. You know, kosher silt, kosher salt! I have . . . never . . . seen . . . one . . . in . . . person!"

Jack overheard Reginald from Old Harbor Academy whisper to his partner, Veronica, "That's the boy from Sieberling School, the crazy one who thinks he can bake."

Thinks he can bake? Jack thought. *You just watch!*

Liz led the group into a room with a large movie screen and rows of leather recliners.

"This is Mr. Farnsworth's private theater," Liz said. "Please be seated."

Liz pressed a button. A twelve-foot-high image of Farnsworth appeared on the screen.

"Darn," Jack said. "He's not here."

"Hello, my young friends. In a few weeks, something stupendous will take place. You, the young bakers of Ardmore, will show your friends, your neighbors, and the world that after seventy-five years, the Bakerstown Bonanza is stronger than ever. I handpicked each of you to represent the Farnsworth tradition of fine baking, and, dare I say, the future of the pastry world. So inspire us! Enthrall us! Bake your little hearts out! You are the very best Ardmore, Ohio, has to offer. Make us all proud!"

After Farnsworth's face disappeared, the contestants jumped to their feet and applauded.

Liz tapped a pen on the clipboard. "To get you better acquainted with your fellow chefs, let's now watch the five-minute videos each of you sent in."

Jack's eyes were transfixed to the screen as the videos played in succession. This would be his first chance to size up the competition. Furiously jotting down notes, he looked for strengths and weaknesses. It soon became apparent that Farnsworth had picked a strong group of foodies who knew how to bake.

This will *be challenging. We'll have to be at the top of our game.*

Jillian's video was the simplest. It began with her standing in Grandma Rita's small kitchen clutching the chipped wooden spoon. Eyes closed, she appeared to be praying as she stirred the batter.

"This spoon is very special to me. It has been in my

143

family for generations. It's what I use when I make rugelach with my bubbe. She's amazing."

A close-up showed two sets of hands kneading the dough into a ball—one pair young and smooth, the other speckled with tan age spots. *The Four Seasons* played in the background.

As Jillian cut the dough into wedges, Grandma Rita stood beside her. They each spread layers of chocolate. While waiting for the rugelach to bake, a montage showed Grandma Rita giving Jillian a golf lesson, changing the oil in her roadster, and replacing a leaky elbow pipe under the kitchen sink.

"I told you my bubbe is amazing!" Jillian said.

The final shot was of Jillian and Grandma Rita holding the plate of rugelach and saying in one voice, *"Bon appetit!"*

Jack glanced at Jillian, who was grasping Grandma Rita's hand as if she never wanted to let it go. Reginald and Veronica snickered as the video ended.

Jack's video played next.

In the kitchen, Jack stared directly into the camera, which shook uncontrollably as if it had been attached to a careening mine cart. The Zombie Brunch song "What's for Dinner?" blasted in the background.

"I rock! I rule! I . . . am . . . unstoppable!" Jack wailed, standing next to his life-size cutout of Farnsworth.

Chad bumped his head on a light fixture and shouted a stream of bleeped-out words.

Jack's head poked above a sea of Farnsworth kitchen gadgets laid out on the counter.

"Time for the *Jack Attack*!" he yelled, clapping his hands and sending a cloud of flour skyward.

Emerging from the puff of white, Jack cracked eggs behind his back, juggled spatulas, and drummed on the counter with palette knives. The music pulsated as he pulled a tray out of the oven.

"Cannolis with pumpkin spice and pistachio filling. Boom!" Jack said, just as Chad tripped over a cord and knocked the mixing bowl to the floor with a crash.

Bleeeeeep.

Jack's father put his hands over his face. Mr. Mermelstein glared at Jack as if he had three heads. Grandma Rita gave Jack a thumbs-up and mouthed, *Yeah, yeah, yeah, yeah, yeah, yeah, yeah!*

Reginald and Veronica pointed at him. "His teammate is Rugelach Girl. We won't have to worry about them," Reginald said.

Jack scribbled one last note: *Do not like Reginald and Veronica.*

Chapter 21

One at a time, Liz and her assistants interviewed each contestant and their families.

"Why is this necessary?" Mr. Fineman sighed. "The contest is about you, not us."

"They use snippets of the videos as background about the contestants as we bake. They show them on three big video screens behind the judging table. At most, you might be on screen for thirty seconds."

Mr. Fineman told the interviewer about Jack's first taste of Boston cream pie and his favorite three words: *YUM! MORE! NOW!*

Mrs. Fineman explained that Jack had a tradition of making her the most irresistible carrot and caramel cupcakes for her birthday. When asked what it meant to have her son as part of the "great Farnsworth baking legacy," she simply said, "No comment." Jack watched as

Bruce lived up to his end of the bet he had made with Jillian.

"Jack . . . makes . . . the . . . best . . . oatmeal . . . cookies . . . in . . . the . . . whole . . . universe," his brother said, choking on every syllable. His voice was so robotic and unconvincing that Jack was certain Bruce's contribution would never be used.

Afterward, Jack and his parents met with Liz to sign the contract.

"Please close the door behind you," Liz said, twiddling with a folder on her desk. Its cover was marked *Jack Fineman Official Profile*. The word *CONFIDENTIAL* was stamped in red ink along the top.

"On behalf of Mr. Farnsworth and everyone at the Bakerstown Bonanza, let me say we're thrilled to have you as a part of the contest's seventy-fifth anniversary."

"Thank you," Mrs. Fineman said, coughing. "It's certainly something we never expected."

"Well, we expect great things from your son."

Liz beamed at Jack.

"As you may know, the success of the Bonanza will depend on more than your skills in the kitchen. Back in the old days, there was no other event like it. Now we're competing against all those reality cooking shows. We need ours to stand above the rest."

"I understand," Jack said. "I'm ready to make it happen!"

"Good. That's why it's important for you to allow your, ah, boisterous personality—the rock 'n' roll attitude—to shine through. The more swagger, the better. It will contrast well with your baking partner's calmer nature. Our research indicates many of our customers will identify with you—the loud guy who speaks his mind and doesn't care what others think. Can you do that?"

"Sure! That's who I am," Jack said.

"Fantastic! Mr. Farnsworth sees a lot of you in himself, Jack," Liz continued. "Someone who isn't afraid to take chances. Someone who won't let anything or anyone stand in the way of a dream."

Hearing Liz talk about Farnsworth and Jack, Mrs. Fineman frowned and looked away. Liz turned to Jack's parents.

"I must say that of all the applications we received, your answers to the questionnaire were the most memorable, especially the cricket cookies."

"Yes, Jack is always thinking of new ingredients to try," Mr. Fineman said. He nervously tugged at his left ear, knowing that it was Jack who had filled out the questionnaire.

"That's good to know," Liz said, looking at Jack. "We just want to make sure there won't be anything out of the ordinary in your recipe. A tarantula trifle might receive a great deal of media attention, but I'm afraid it will never end up on the cover of the cookbook. Understand?"

"Loud and clear," Jack said.

Jillian and her family entered Liz's office next.

"I'm glad you could all be here today," Liz said. "We are delighted to have you as a contestant, Jillian. Your video was lovely."

Jillian nodded. Liz turned to Grandma Rita.

"And it is an honor to meet you in person. Everyone on the staff wishes they had a Grandma Rita in their lives."

"Or a granddaughter like Jillian," Grandma Rita said.

"I agree," Liz said. "It's the reason she was selected. Our test audiences adored her. We think Jillian could become a sensation!"

"A sensation? I don't understand," Mr. Mermelstein said. "And who is *we*?"

Liz opened a folder with Jillian's name on it.

"We don't choose anyone without first doing a thorough background check. Mr. Farnsworth doesn't like surprises. Neither do our lawyers."

Jillian gulped hard. She felt like a pawn about to be moved to a dangerous square on a chessboard.

"During our research, Jillian, we found you weren't entirely honest on your application. While not untruthful, you left out one significant detail."

"What detail?" Mr. Mermelstein asked, gripping the arms of his chair and knowing full well what Liz meant.

"Your wife . . . Jillian's mother."

"As you can imagine," he said through gritted teeth, "some things are too personal to share with the world. And,

149

honestly, I don't appreciate you snooping around like that."

"It's just standard procedure, Mr. Mermelstein. As you know, there's quite a bit you can discover just by doing a simple Google search."

"Such as?" Grandma Rita asked.

From the folder Liz pulled out an article from *The Seattle Times* about the opening of Joan of Hearts Pastry Shop. In the photo, Jillian's mother held up the tiger maple spoon. A second clipping showed a photo of Jillian and her mother passing out jelly-filled donuts at a menorah-lighting celebration at the mall. The final article was about the memorial service held at the pastry shop in honor of her mother. A photo showed Jillian clutching the wooden spoon to her chest.

"Please understand, Mr. Mermelstein. We *are* looking out for Jillian's best interests."

"I fail to see how," he snorted.

"The Bakerstown Bonanza is about real people—their stories, their dreams, their hopes, their motivations. We believe Jillian's life will connect with the people who for generations have used Farnsworth sugar and baking utensils. But we are certain they will love her more if they knew her whole story. This is *very* important."

Jillian imagined strangers sifting through her private memory box like shoppers rummaging through knickknacks at a garage sale. She thought about the ten thousand phones recording her as she talked about the peaceful Saturday mornings she spent with her mother. She pictured herself breaking down on camera, sharing her sorrow with people as they scrolled through social media while waiting in line at the grocery store, the post office—everywhere. And the Bonanza could use her words and these images—however they wanted to—in perpetuity. Forever.

I can't do it, she thought. *I just can't.*

"It hasn't even been a year since . . ." Mr. Mermelstein trailed off. "Our loss is too recent and too painful. I don't want my daughter to have complete strangers pestering her about a tragic memory, to have baking, the one thing that brings her complete joy, be tainted and ruined. No amount of money in the world is worth that."

"I understand," Liz said. "Still, I strongly encourage Jillian to mention her mother during the event. This comes straight from Phineas Farnsworth III himself. While there are no guarantees, doing so *will* greatly increase Jillian's chances of winning. And Mr. Farnsworth has bigger plans for Jillian."

"What plans?" Grandma Rita asked.

"He thinks Jillian has potential to be the face of his new line of 'Little Hands with Big Appetites' junior baking products. Your granddaughter could be a star."

"Why me?" Jillian blurted out. "I'm not special."

"Oh, but you are," Liz said. "You have the look and the personality Mr. Farnsworth wants. He's convinced you are perfect for the role. And he's never wrong when it comes to business. This would change your life."

"How?" Jillian asked.

"You and your family would travel the world. Your image would be everywhere—television commercials, the Internet, and billboards in Times Square. Someday you may even have your own show. Mr. Farnsworth can make all of this happen—and more!"

Liz reached behind her desk and pulled out a stack of art boards. They were mock-ups of advertisements showing a girl using a Farnsworth Junior Food Processor. Jillian's head had been photoshopped to the girl's body. The slogan above the food processor read, *The next best thing to my mother's wooden spoon.*

"Our graphic design department put these together," Liz said. "It is Mr. Farnsworth's idea for the campaign. With your permission, of course, we would begin running this and other ads using actual photos." Liz looked at Mr. Mermelstein. "You would never have to worry about money again."

"And if she doesn't go along?" Mr. Mermelstein asked, his voice wavering.

"All I can say is Mr. Farnsworth doesn't like to be disappointed."

Chapter 22

ack spent the next day compiling his own profiles of the other contestants in his scrapbook:

Team 1

Contestant 1: Quentin Lindenberg

School: Feldspar Math and Science Institute

The Video: All about animals. Has two border collies, five cats, a parakeet, and a three-legged rescue ferret named Fergus. Bakes treats for his pets. Made pecan pie brownies to raise money for Ardmore's Animal Adoption Shelter. Last scene shows him feeding a two-week-old kitten with a bottle.

Contestant 2: Marcia Thorne

School: Feldspar Math and Science Institute

The Video: Helps out taking care of her triplet brothers.

Made them each a cake for their first birthdays—carrot, raspberry, and red velvet with beet juice. Interesting choices! Some of the prize money will go toward the triplets' college fund. Has won the blue ribbon for pie making in the junior division at the Ardmore County Fair every year since second grade.

About the School: Kids who go to Feldspar are ultra brainy, ultra serious, and DO NOT LIKE TO LOSE. They will be tough to beat.

Team 2

Contestant 1: Veronica Hartman
School: Old Harbor Academy
The Video: Bakes shoofly pie with residents at the Ardmore Nursing Home. I can almost taste the molasses. Learned to bake from a French au pair who studied at the La Cuisine Paris Culinary Institute. Wants to start her own cooking school. Owns all the latest baking gadgets. Mentions Farnsworth products six times in the video.

Contestant 2: Reginald Nestland
School: Old Harbor Academy
The Video: Turns desserts into works of art. Created and decorated sheet cakes of American Gothic and the Mona Lisa plus a portrait of Farnsworth. I'm not sure how they taste, but the presentation is amazing. His

dream is to make an edible replica of the Sistine Chapel ceiling.

About the School: Old Harbor Academy has stomped on Sieberling School in every event for the last fifty years. Rumor: The school's PTA flew in world-famous pastry chef Francois Furveau to coach Reginald and Veronica. They will be really tough to beat.

Team 3
Contestant 1: Jillian Mermelstein
School: Sieberling School
The Video: Not flashy, but it got Farnsworth's attention. She is an excellent competitor who has the coolest grandma ever. Problem: She wants to make something simple for the contest, which is a huge mistake!

Contestant 2: Me
School: Sieberling School
The Video: This is who they want me to be. I'm ready for it! According to Ms. Escobar, Mr. Farnsworth likes me! That is a big deal! Problem: Jillian doesn't agree with my idea for a layer cake using the top four flavors of the past winning recipes. I _must_ convince her before the big day.

About Our School: I want to be Sieberling's hero. That

sure would impress Amy Eppington! Ms. Riedel may even skip the next grammar lesson. The school's trophy case is filled with participation awards and "better luck next time" plaques. Jillian and I will do our best to change that!

Jack analyzed his notes, made some calculations, flipped through his scrapbook for the thousandth time, and had a heart-to-heart chat with his Phineas Farnsworth III life-size cutout. He could tell why Farnsworth selected the other contestants: kittens, nursing homes, adorable triplets, his portrait, and an incredible bubbe.

So why did he pick me? I know! It's because I'm just like him! He sees a big future for me! It won't be easy, but Jillian and I can win the Bakerstown Bonanza! I'm sure of it!

Chapter 23

L iz emailed the contestants and their families the schedule for the weekend event:

Saturday, May 1 (Ardmore Heritage Day Festival)

1. Arrive at the Culinary Arts Pavilion at the Ardmore County Fairgrounds (to the right of the Goat Barn) at 8 a.m. You will receive the official Bonanza chef's hat and apron you will be required to wear at all times.

2. The press conference for contestants and their families will begin at 9 a.m. Be prepared to answer questions about yourself and your baking background.

3. The Ardmore Heritage Parade will begin at 1 p.m. at the fairground entrance. You will be riding on the Farnsworth Company float. At the end of the

parade, you must be available to greet the public and sign autographs.

Sunday, May 2 (Bonanza Day!)

1. The Bakerstown Bonanza begins at 10 a.m. in the auditorium of the Samuel P. Ardmore Convention Center. (See map.) Basic ingredients such as sugar, butter, eggs, and milk will be provided. You are responsible for bringing all other special ingredients required to make your recipe.

2. All contestants will bring one special item from home to help them in the contest. Prior to baking, you will give a short speech about the item. After baking, you will explain the recipe to Mr. Farnsworth.

3. Contestants will have three hours to make their creation. Judging will take place promptly at 2 p.m.

4. Prizes will be awarded once Mr. Farnsworth has tested and approved the winning recipe.

Best of luck!

Jack, Jillian, and Chad scanned Liz's email. Jillian felt queasy about participating in the press conference and speaking at the Bonanza. Jack practically vibrated with excitement at the thought of finally meeting his idol.

Chad pointed out the obvious problem his friends had yet to solve: "It says you're responsible for bringing any special ingredients. How will you know what those are if you haven't selected a recipe?"

The Sieberling School teammates shrugged. Neither would budge on what they believed was the best choice: Jillian wanted to make the chocolate rugelach from her mother's recipe book; Jack wanted to bake a four-layer cake.

"Yours is too big," Jillian argued.

"Yours is too small," Jack shot back.

"Stop sounding like Goldilocks!" Chad said.

"I know I'm right," Jack said firmly. "My scrapbook does not lie."

"No, your scrapbook is wrong!" Jillian said, holding up the tattered recipe book and glaring at Jack.

Chad stepped in between them.

"Okay, you two. Enough arguing! I have an idea. Let's do a baking challenge like on those reality shows."

"What?" Jack said.

"I'll give you a challenge to bake something as a team. Whatever you come up with will be your recipe for the contest. This will force you to make a choice."

"Chad's right," Jillian said. "If we don't have a recipe, we don't have a chance."

"I don't know," Jack said.

"Look, to sweeten the deal I'll do the interpretive beehive dance—in front of the entire school—if you'll do this."

"How can you turn down that offer, Jack?" Jillian asked.

"Fine, I'm in," Jack agreed.

"Super!" Chad said. "Let's get started. I'll pretend to be Francois Furveau from the Fab Food Network."

He paused for a moment before speaking in a screechy French accent: "Zee team from Zieberling School will make . . . an off-ze-wall cake! Surprise me! Delight me! Go nutty! It doesn't even have to make sense! The zanier, the better! Work together and zee what happens. You must complete zis task in one, two, three hours!"

"An off-the-wall cake?" Jack said.

"Hey, I'm no foodie, bro. It was the only thing I could think of," Chad said. "I mean, do not question zee great Francois Furveau! YOU WILL DO AS I COMMAND! I will set zee timer. Now . . . start your burners!"

Jack stared blankly into an empty mixing bowl. His mind was equally empty—all the analysis from his scrapbook hopelessly locked deep in his brain.

Zany? There is no pie chart for zany!

With only days until the contest, Jack feared the moment he had waited for his whole life was crumbling around him. It had been easy watching the Bakerstown Bonanza from the safety of the front row. He never imagined it would be so hard when the pressure was on. Jillian tried to snap him out of his trance.

"Do you still have any crickets stashed in the cupboard?" she asked.

"Not funny," Jack replied.

Jack glanced up to see Bruce walking out of his bedroom door. He was wearing his most outrageous pair of golf pants yet—canary yellow and purple paisley squares with emerald diamond accents.

That's when it hit him.

"Pants!" Jack exclaimed. "Bruce's golfing pants! What's crazier than that for a cake?"

He raced to the pantry and grabbed what he needed.

As Jack went to work, Jillian looked at Bruce and remembered Chad's instructions: *It doesn't even have to make sense.*

Not everything in life is supposed to make sense, she thought.

"Got it!" Jillian said, bolting to the cupboard and returning with an armful of ingredients. "You handle the cake. I'll take care of the decorations."

"Sounds good," Jack said as he measured out cups of flour.

Jillian turned to her mother's recipe for shortbread cookies. She mixed the batter and poured it into a pan. Once baked and cooled, she smoothed on white icing and cut it into tiny squares about the size of postage stamps.

Jack pulled his cake out of the oven, let it cool, and then iced it in a checkered pattern using every color he could remember from Bruce's pants collection.

Jillian blocked out everything but the sound of her beating heart. Using a black edible marker, she wrote

161

alphabet letters on each square and randomly arranged them on top of Jack's checkered-pants icing.

"For Dad," Jillian whispered.

"One last touch in honor of Chad," Jack said, tossing a handful of blue and gold sprinkles onto the cake.

The buzzer sounded.

Jack and Jillian took deep breaths.

"Good job, partner," Jack said, giving her a high five.

"It's perfectly imperfect," Jillian said.

"Monsieur Furveau, we present to you our Mixed-Up Scrabble Babble Cake," Jack said with a flourish.

Chad took a bite of the cake, which was divided into four sections—maple, banana, coconut, and vanilla. Then he popped two shortbread Scrabble tiles into his mouth. His eyes rolled back in his head as he savored the cookies.

"Say magic feet," Chad said.

"You mean, *C'est magnifique*. It means, 'It's magnificent' in French," Jillian said.

"Well, it's better than magnificent," Chad said. "It will be the winning recipe! You did it! I knew you could!"

"Two words," Jillian said.

"I know. I know. Beehive dance."

As Jillian looked at the letters on top of the cake, she realized her life was still a jumble. She wanted to tell Jack what Liz had said: Talk about your mother and your chance of winning increases. Stay silent, disappoint Phineas

Farnsworth III, and leave with nothing. No money for your family. No Culinary Education Center for the school. No recipe on the cover of the Farnsworth cookbook. She wondered how Jack would react if he knew. Would he force her to tell? And how would Jack feel learning that Farnsworth wanted *her* to be on his billboards and star in his commercials?

No more secrets, she vowed.

"Jack, I have something to say . . ."

"One sec, Jillian. Now that we have a recipe, we're going to beat Old Harbor and Feldspar!" he said, showing Jillian his notes on the contestants. "I thought I'd have to wait seven years for my dream to come true. And when we win, this will be big for me, I mean, for us. Sorry, what did you want to say?"

"Never mind. It's not important."

I just can't tell Jack the truth, not right now, she thought. *It would destroy him, and the Bonanza hasn't even begun.*

Jillian reached down and arranged three letters on top of the cake to form the word *MOM*.

I wish you were here. You'd know what to do.

Chapter 24

ack, his parents, and Bruce milled about in the Culinary Arts Pavilion. The other contestants and their families sipped coffee and picked at breakfast pastries as they awaited the start of the press conference. No one was more jittery than Jack.

In minutes, his idol would be standing near the apricot croissants offering his warmest welcome and, as Jack hoped, entertaining them with anecdotes about his days growing up in Ardmore.

Jack had stayed up half the night practicing exactly what he would say when shaking Phineas Farnsworth III's hand: *I have dreamed about being in the Bakerstown Bonanza my whole life. I will not disappoint you.*

Then Jack imagined Farnsworth's reply as he put his arm around his shoulder like a favorite uncle. *I can't wait to see what you bake.*

Each contestant wore identical aprons and chef's hats. The slogan, *Little Hands with Big Appetites*, was emblazoned in purple thread across the front of each apron. The hats bore the Farnsworth company logo.

Before Farnsworth and the media arrived, Liz gave the contestants a short pep talk. "Today's press conference is as important as the baking tomorrow. Mr. Farnsworth, at great expense, has placed cameras around the pavilion to capture you at every possible angle. We don't want to miss a moment."

Liz stopped as Phineas Farnsworth III swept through the door. He wore his usual three-piece pinstriped suit and hand-stitched Italian shoes Jack recognized from a photograph he had seen in *Forbes* magazine.

"Those cost twenty thousand dollars. The heels are encrusted with real diamonds," Jack said to his mother.

Farnsworth opened his arms wide and addressed the contestants.

"Let me welcome you all to the seventy-fifth anniversary of the Bakerstown Bonanza," he boomed. "I assume this will be your first time talking to the press. My advice—be yourself. The camera is *not* your enemy. Think of it as your best friend and be ready to reveal your true self. Show your emotions. Have fun. And above all, let the world see who you are and why you deserve to be here."

Farnsworth looked directly at Jillian and spoke slowly and clearly. "Don't forget, we're here to put on a good show."

I will. Don't you worry about that, she thought.

Reporters trickled into the pavilion. Soon every seat was occupied. Jack recognized the food critic from *The New York Times* and writers from every major gourmet magazine and blog. News crews from the local station, cable channels like the Fab Food Network, and even CNN were there.

Jillian looked out at the sea of media, shocked by the amount of people who would be capturing her every word. No fewer than six television cameras swiveled toward the long table where she and the other contestants waited to be poked and prodded. Family members sat on folding chairs behind them.

The contestants stood, said their name and school, and introduced their guests.

When it was Jack's turn, he didn't hold back:

"Jack Fineman is in the house, folks! Give it up! Behind me is the whole fam—my dad, mom, and my older brother, Bruce."

From down the table, Jack heard Reginald and Veronica let out a simultaneous cackle, followed by "Jinx!"

"Look . . . at . . . those . . . pants!" Reginald whispered loud enough to be picked up by the microphone. Some reporters chuckled. Everyone turned toward Bruce, who fought back tears.

Jack paused. He found it strange to see his brother, for once, on the hurtful side of the teasing equation. He watched as Bruce melted under the hot lights, every camera and phone pointed in the direction of his multihued slacks. He heard the crowd's guffaws begin to swell. It only took a moment for Jack to decide what to do.

"Go ahead and laugh," he snarled. "But in a few years you'll be watching my brother on the Golf Channel winning millions of dollars. He rocks at golf! And his pants rock, too!"

Jillian gave Jack a slight grin.

"With that out of the way, we're ready for our first question," Farnsworth said.

A correspondent from *Chef's Monthly* asked, "While I'm sure you don't want to reveal too much about your recipe, could you tell us a little about your strategy for winning? What gives you the edge over your competition? And who inspires you?"

Quentin Lindenberg from Feldspar Math and Science Institute gave a quick answer.

"Baking is really very simple," he said. "Every ingredient must be measured exactly and blended with the others at the precise moment. There is no room for error. One extra granule of salt could disrupt the recipe's delicate balance. You won't find Marcia and me adding a pinch of anything. We believe in magic—the magic of chemistry."

"Quentin and I have been chemistry partners since third grade," Marcia added. "What we will bake tomorrow will be based on hours and hours spent together in the lab, uh, kitchen. To create a successful recipe, you must understand how carbohydrates, proteins, and fats work together."

"In less technical terms, our dessert will be really yummy," Quentin said as the pool of reporters laughed.

Veronica of Old Harbor Academy spoke next.

"Reginald and I have carefully studied the great chefs of the world. Last year Old Harbor offered a summer seminar in 'The History of French Pastries' based on the book by the great Francois Furveau. It was our honor to meet him in person. He has been a huge help to us."

I knew it, Jack thought.

"We know this event is important to our school, to our city, and to the long legacy of pastry chefs far and wide," Reginald said. "Our strategy is to approach the contest with the same attitude as we approach everything at Old Harbor—coming in second place is not an option. Failure is not part of our vocabulary. Our dessert will be like nothing the contest has ever seen—a true work of art. As Francois Furveau says, 'If Rembrandt were alive today, he'd be decorating cupcakes.' We can't wait for tomorrow."

Jack jumped up.

"We can't wait, either!" he shouted. "Not to trash-talk the other schools, but Sieberling is going to dominate this event. Guaranteed! Forget chemistry formulas and the *great* Francois Furveau. I know more about the Bakerstown Bonanza than anyone alive, other than

Phineas Farnsworth III. Go on, ask me anything."

"Jack, please," Jillian whispered.

From the back, a reporter shouted, "Who won the contest in 1957?"

"Easy peasy. Blaire Tremont from Madison, Wisconsin. She made a blueberry cheesecake. The runner-up was Cindy Strassford from Lexington, Kentucky, with a caramel flan topped with figs. Boom! Is that the best you've got?"

Another reporter started to speak when Farnsworth interrupted.

"I'm afraid Jillian Mermelstein hasn't had the opportunity to answer the first question. Tell us, Jillian, what is your strategy for winning?"

"To do my best," she said.

Farnsworth continued.

"Is there anyone special you'll be thinking about as you bake? Anyone who has inspired you?"

"Yes, actually two people, my father and Grandma Rita," she said, pointing behind her.

"How lovely," Farnsworth said, his face growing red with anger. "Is there someone else who you wish could be here with you today?"

Sorry, memory box closed, Jillian thought.

"No. But thank you for asking."

Farnsworth persisted.

"Don't be coy. Tell us about that special person who inspires you."

Jillian looked at the reporters and cameras. She glanced back at her father and Grandma Rita.

"Well, I guess you could say you've inspired me."

"Excuse me?"

"You've shown me the importance of standing up for what I believe no matter how much somebody pushes you around," Jillian said.

Farnsworth's face turned the color of an overripe tomato about to implode in the hot sun.

As the press conference continued, Jack conducted himself as Liz had instructed. He sang his favorite Zombie Brunch song, juggled spatulas, and shouted out a school cheer he and Chad had written: "Roses are red, violets are blue, if you're not a Fighting Mustang, I feel sorry for you!"

"That went pretty well," Jack said to Jillian afterward. "But I wonder why Farnsworth looks so angry."

"No idea, Jack. Come on, we're supposed to be in the parade."

Chad texted Jack:

> Dude! How did the press conference go?

> It was cool!

> Did you juggle the spatulas?

170

You bet!

Did you get a selfie with
the Big Guy?

He's too busy. Maybe later.

See you at the parade.

Phineas Farnsworth III and the mayor led the Ardmore Heritage Parade riding in the back of a Rolls-Royce convertible. A float followed holding past Bonanza winners. The crowd lined both sides of Market Street, waving and cheering as a team of dancing horses, the city's fleet of fire trucks, and kids dressed like spoons and forks strode by. The Ardmore High School marching band played the bouncy tune of the 1940s radio jingle, "F Is for Fun, Food, and Farnsworth." Over and over again.

Jillian, Jack, and the other contestants rode on the Farnsworth company float—a huge mixing bowl sitting on a flatbed truck decorated to resemble a kitchen countertop. They perched on the rim and tossed sample bags of Farnsworth Semi-Sweet Chocolate Chips to the crowd. An updated version of the Farnsworth jingle from the 1980s blasted from speakers painted to resemble boxes of baking soda:

Farnsworth puts the fun in food
So if you're in a foodie mood
Be a righteous gal or dude
And bake with Farnsworth attitude!

After the parade, the contestants signed autographs and posed for publicity photos. Liz met the six bakers back at the fairgrounds for final instructions.

"Are you ready for tomorrow?" she asked.

"Yes," they all moaned, exhausted from the strain of smiling throughout the day.

"Wonderful. My team and I have taken the liberty of writing brief scripts for each of you. That will be one less thing you'll have to worry about. No thanks necessary. I suggest you memorize it. The words will also appear on a teleprompter."

Liz handed out the scripts. Jack glanced at his.

Mr. Farnsworth: All of our bakers were allowed to bring one item to help them. And what did you bring?

Jack: The choice was obvious. I brought my Farnsworth Magic Rolling Pin Junior. It flattens dough without the fuss thanks to its sure-grip handles that won't slip or slide.

Mr. Farnsworth: Another fine pick!

"This will be easy," Jack said to Jillian. "All I have to do is talk about one of Farnsworth's products. What does yours say?"

Jillian scanned her sheet.

"Same as yours, Jack."

"Secondly, be at the convention center at nine o'clock sharp," Liz continued. "Now go home, rehearse your lines, and get a good night's sleep."

"How am I going to sleep?" Jack said. "After tomorrow, we'll be the heroes of Sieberling School and our recipe will be on the cover of the *Farnsworth Best of the Bonanza* cookbook. We'll . . . be . . . world . . . famous."

"Jack—"

"I apologize. I was wrong about us. We *do* make a great team. Jack and Jillian—the grand prize winners of the seventy-fifth Bakerstown Bonanza!"

Jillian tried to tell Jack the truth, but her lips failed to form the words. She felt like Phineas Farnsworth III, holding Jack's fate in her hands.

She looked down at the script and thought about her father.

What am I going to do?

Chapter 25

While the contestants' families chatted in the fairgrounds parking lot, Jack sneaked off to get a selfie with Phineas Farnsworth III.

He moved quietly through the empty midway, past the dunking booth and the bumper car ride. Everyone had left for the day. Liz spotted him as he drew closer to the Culinary Arts Pavilion where the press conference had been held.

"I'm glad I ran into you," she said, breathlessly. "I've been looking for you everywhere. There's somebody rather important who would like a few words with you."

"You mean . . ."

"Yes, Mr. Farnsworth asked me to find you. He's a busy man, so consider yourself very fortunate. He told me he wanted a few minutes to get to know you personally."

This . . . is . . . not . . . happening!

Jack wobbled on his feet. "He wants to meet *me*? I was just going to see if I could get a selfie with him. My parents are waiting . . ."

"This won't take long. Like I said, he doesn't have much time to spare."

Liz led Jack to a long wooden structure on the edge of the fairgrounds. A carved sign over the door read, *4-H Building*. From the front stoop, Jack smelled the pungent odors of deep-fried pickles and sheep manure, which were wafting from a nearby barn. His heart thumped hard as he pushed open the door and walked to the back of the cavernous, dimly lit space, where Farnsworth sat at a card table, hunched over and cloaked in shadows.

Farnsworth stood up as Jack approached. All six feet and six inches of him loomed over the starstruck boy. He gave Jack a firm handshake, the kind business leaders use to finalize an important deal. Jack winced as Farnsworth's enormous hand squeezed his own.

"Please sit down, Jack," Farnsworth said in a silky tone, far different from what Jack had heard during his television interviews. "So glad Liz was able to corral you. I wanted to compliment you in person on your outstanding performance today during the press conference. A video of you juggling spatulas has already gone viral. More than one hundred thousand views in a little more than two hours. You're famous already, young man!"

"Really?" Jack said, the word escaping from his mouth

in a nervous whisper. He still couldn't believe Farnsworth was right in front of him!

"Yes, Jack. One . . . hundred . . . thousand. And that's just the tip of the iceberg. With your assistance, this could be our most successful Bonanza ever."

"You can count on me," Jack said.

"Superb. I knew I could." He held up some sheets of paper Jack recognized as his application to the Bonanza. "It says here that you own a life-size cardboard cutout of me. Ah yes, I do recall seeing that in your video as well. I'd have to say that while I've received hundreds of honors over my career, no one has ever rescued me from a trash bin at their local Food Mart. I'm flattered."

"It's by my bed," Jack said. "It kind of creeps my parents out, but—"

Farnsworth interrupted. "It also appears that fame is of great importance to you. That's good. It's what drives people like us. It's fuel for our engines. Food for our souls. But as you'll learn, there are no guarantees in life. Simply wanting fame is not enough."

"I don't understand."

"Of course you don't." Farnsworth chuckled. "Let me ask: How does one rise to the top of the baking world? Why do some pastry chefs end up perched atop a six-tiered cake while others flounder in the bottom of the mixing bowl? By having life-sized dreams—like yours. And by not letting anything or anyone stand in the way of achieving them."

"Gotta dream big. Gotta dream big," Jack said, gaining confidence.

"Smart boy. I'd say you're well on your way. And from your video, it's rather clear to me you have a fine chance of winning the Bonanza. I could almost taste your cannolis with pumpkin spice and pistachio filling. I might even have to steal the recipe," he said, letting out a laugh.

No way! Phineas Farnsworth III liked my cannolis. Boom!

"Just wait until tomorrow. Jillian and I will be making something even better for the Bonanza!"

Farnsworth rose from the chair and slowly began pacing around Jack. His expensive shoes echoed off the concrete floor.

"Ah, Jillian. *She's* the problem—the fly in the batter. The one standing in your way."

"Jillian's not a problem," Jack said, confused. "She's an incredible baker."

"That may be true, but she has refused to honor my simple . . . innocent . . . harmless request to talk about her mother. I instructed Liz to make this crystal clear to Jillian, and she blew her chance at the press conference."

"But why does it matter?" Jack asked. "We're going to rule at the contest tomorrow whether she talks about her mother or not!"

"The Bonanza is about more than baking. Our contestants' stories are equally important. And Jillian has a great one to tell about how she learned to bake. But she is unwilling to share it. How could anyone throw away so much for so little?"

So little? Jack thought. *It's not little to Jillian.*

"How do you know about her mother?" Jack asked.

"Oh, you can learn a lot from a simple Google search."

Jack didn't know what to say.

"You need to convince Jillian to talk about her mother . . . the wooden spoon . . . her memories. Doing so will truly make this the greatest Bonanza in our seventy-five-year history. You can make this happen. Plus, there's one more thing."

"What's that?"

"It will help *your* chances of winning."

"You mean if Jillian does what you ask . . ."

"As I said, there are no guarantees in life, but yes," Farnsworth said, winking. "Imagine this—the Culinary Education Center for your school, seventy-five thousand dollars in your pocket, and all the fame an eleven-year-old from Ardmore, Ohio, could ever handle."

Jack sat mesmerized by Farnsworth's hypnotic voice— the same one he used on his commercials to persuade bakers to purchase every glimmering gadget the company produced. Farnsworth continued to prowl around the table.

"I see myself in you, Jack. Your dreams are too big for this small town. In fact, if it were up to me, I'd take Ardmore apart brick by brick and rebuild it from the ground up. Many years ago, the city let me tear down some old buildings on a couple of streets and no one seemed to mind. I'm sure that once you've opened your Fineman's Fine Pastry Shops in New York, Paris, and Rome, you won't think twice about Ardmore."

"Fineman's Fine Pastry Shops?"

"That's just a name I came up with off the top of my head. It helps to know people who operate a successful business, people who can get you started off on the right foot. For example, you might need a logo for your pastry shops someday. I employ the finest art department in the food industry."

"You mean you would help me?"

"That all depends . . ." Farnsworth glanced at his watch. "On that note, I must move on to other matters. I trust you will keep our little chat between us."

"Yes, oh, yes," Jack said, edging toward the door. "It was nice meeting you."

"You as well, my boy. Remember our deal about Jillian. A good friend like you can help her make a smart decision— one that can benefit you both."

Standing by the exit, Jack blurted out the lines he had rehearsed over and over the night before. "I have dreamed about being in the Bakerstown Bonanza my whole life. I will not disappoint you."

Jack bolted from the 4-H Building, leaving a trail of dust in his wake. He sprinted through the silent rows of carnival rides and concession stands, a swirl of thoughts ping-ponging inside his head.

One hundred thousand views! Farnsworth liked my cannolis! Fineman's Fine Pastry Shops! Paris, Rome, New York! You may need a logo. A good friend like you. It will help your chances. That all depends . . .

Jack zoomed into the parking lot. He frantically flung open his parents' car door to find Jillian sitting quietly in the backseat.

"Hi, Jack. My dad has to get to work and Grandma Rita has a meeting at the university, so your mom offered to drive me home," she said, scanning Jack's face. "Hey, is everything alright? You look kind of . . . frazzled."

"Fine. I'm fine. Can we just go?" Jack begged, trying to make sense of his meeting with Farnsworth.

How am I going to convince Jillian?

Liz entered the 4-H Building as Farnsworth brushed dust off his suit jacket.

"How did it go?" she asked.

"Very well, as I expected. I believe our issue with Jillian is resolved. I take it that you've handled the necessary details on your end?"

"Yes, I gave her the script you wrote."

"Good. Jillian has one final chance. All she has to do is talk about her mother and that spoon on camera. We'll rerun the video of her confession so many times in our advertisements that every man, woman, and child from Ohio to Australia will be able to recite her speech by heart."

"Then what?"

"Jack and Jillian win. And I sell five million Junior Cookie Scoops in less than a week. End of story."

"What if she doesn't cooperate?"

"That will not be a problem. I guarantee it."

Chapter 26

On the ride home from the fairgrounds, Jack realized that Jillian had not told him the whole truth again.

Farnsworth asked Jillian to talk about her mother! Jack thought. *Why didn't she tell me? I thought we were partners? Did she think I would force her to share her mother's story? Then again, would bringing up her mother be such a big deal? Maybe just once or twice? Think of all that we'll lose if she doesn't.*

Still under Farnsworth's spell from the meeting, he made a decision: *As Jillian's friend, it's up to me to help her make the right choice about the Bonanza—for both of us.*

After a few minutes of silence, Jack eased into the conversation.

"Big day tomorrow," he said.

"Massive," Jillian replied. She looked out the window

at the rows of office buildings zipping by in downtown Ardmore.

"I know we're ready for the Bonanza. We've made the Mixed-Up Scrabble Babble Cake so many times we could blend the ingredients in our sleep. The competition is going to be tough, though. We'll need every edge we can get to win. One slip and, boom, Old Harbor or Feldspar takes home the top prize."

"What do you mean, 'edge'?" Jillian asked, peering closely at Jack.

"You know, anything that would make Farnsworth choose us over the other teams."

Jillian turned away. For days she had considered telling Jack the truth. She wrestled with the hard fact that she hadn't decided what she would do tomorrow in front of the microphone with Farnsworth glaring at her on stage. Talking about her mother would give them an edge, but would that be fair to the other contestants? The money would change her family's life . . . and Jack would get to live out his dream. But . . . there were so many *buts* to think about . . .

"Let's bake our very best and see what happens," Jillian said, still unable to tell Jack the complete story.

"If you can think of *anything* that will give us an advantage, now's your chance," Jack said. "I know you don't like Farnsworth, but he's really not such a bad guy."

"What makes you say that?"

"Just a feeling I get," Jack said, looking down at the bumpy brick street passing by. "He's counting on us to put on a good show tomorrow. We probably should do what he asks."

"What do you mean?"

"Easy things, like reading the scripts Liz gave us about his new products. Stuff like that. The smoother everything goes, the easier it will be for us to bake—and win!"

"Right . . ."

Jack pulled out a bag of Farnsworth Semi-Sweet Chocolate Chips, took a handful and offered the rest to Jillian. He dumped half of them in her hand.

"Thanks," she said. "It was a long day. I must have signed a hundred autographs after the parade."

"Me too," Jack said. "Any strange requests?"

"Well, you know that fourth-grader who had me sign his corn chip?"

"Yes! How could I forget?"

"He was there asking for another autograph."

"He must really think you're going to be famous."

"Actually, he needed a replacement chip because . . ." She couldn't finish the sentence.

"Because?"

"His little brother ate it," she said, letting out a burst of laughter. "Thought it was just a regular corn chip sitting on his brother's nightstand."

"Did you sign it?"

"Yeah, but it cost him three dollars," she said, producing three crisp bills from her pocket and letting out another laugh. Jack joined her. Soon they were giggling as hard as they had in Ms. Riedel's class during their science project.

After the laughter faded, Jillian gave Jack a serious look. "I need to tell you something."

This is it, Jack thought. *She's going to say that she'll talk about her mother at the Bonanza! We can't lose. Boom!*

"Is it about the contest?" Jack asked, hopefully.

"No, it's way more important. I wanted to thank you for being my friend. That's all."

Before Jack could respond, the car hit a dip in the brick street, violently jarring him in the backseat. He looked out the window as the baking supply factory came into view. Reeling from the jolt, he began recalling details of his meeting with Farnsworth—things he had pushed to the back of his mind.

"Oooh," Jillian said. "This is where Maple Street intersects with Market Street."

Old buildings torn down, Jack thought.

"I read about it in my research about the company. Farnsworth expanded the business here in 1980," Jillian continued.

Jack's mind was on overdrive. *And no one seemed to mind.*

Jillian went on. "He had a bunch of old shops demolished . . ."

"Brick by brick," Jack said out loud, staring at the Maple and Market streets sign—the same one in the photo of Goldfarb Bakery just hours before it was destroyed. His brain clicked, as if the final piece of a long-unsolved puzzle snapped into place.

"STOP THE CAR!" he screamed.

Mrs. Fineman slammed on the brakes. Jack jumped out of the car and ran to the building nearest the street sign. Jillian followed. "What are you doing, Jack?" she asked.

"*Warehouse—Farnsworth Baking Supply Company,*" Jack read aloud from the black-and-white sign atop the building. It featured the cartoonish drawing of Farnsworth in a chef's hat, giving a thumbs-up.

Jack closed his eyes and imagined the smell of chocolate rugelach drifting out of the curtained windows of Goldfarb Bakery. He saw Bubbe Leah holding a tray of macaroons pulled fresh from the oven. He heard the sound of a wrecking ball and the last brick striking the pavement with a thud.

"This is where the Goldfarb Bakery used to stand," Jack explained. "My great-grandparents Leah and Stan owned it. The city allowed Farnsworth to take the property so he could expand the business. My mom says that once the shop was gone, her grandmother was never the same. Her days of making lemon babkas and chocolate rugelach for her customers were over."

"I'm so sorry, Jack," Jillian said.

"Remember how I said that chocolate rugelach wasn't good enough for the Bonanza? I've changed my mind. We *have* to make chocolate rugelach."

"Why?"

"It's something we need to do."

Once home, Jack grabbed his life-size Phineas Farnsworth III cutout, chucked it into his closet, and slammed the door.

"And don't come out until I tell you!" he yelled, falling on the bed.

Jack felt betrayed. It was far worse than realizing that Jillian's chocolate rugelach was better than his butterscotch basil brownies. His dreams of becoming the next big thing from Ardmore had been shattered. Not only did he *not* want to *be* Farnsworth, but the mere thought of the city's most famous resident made his stomach churn.

Grabbing a box, Jack started filling it with everything emblazoned with the Farnsworth logo. When the first box could hold no more, he did the same with a second and a third. He threw a blanket over his seventy-four copies of the *Farnsworth Best of the Bonanza* cookbooks. The Bonanza chef's hat went into the trash can followed by the apron that read *Little Hands with Big Appetites*.

"What are you doing, Jack?" Mrs. Fineman asked, standing in the doorway.

Can't stop. There's work to be done, Jack thought. Wherever he turned, another Farnsworth product needed to be removed from his sight.

"Jack! Talk to me!"

"Mom, Farnsworth is a big fake. Jillian was right. He *is* mean. And he doesn't really like Ardmore! Why didn't you tell me Farnsworth tore down the family's bakery shop? I'm not going to be in the Bonanza. In fact, I'm never baking again. I'm done."

Mrs. Fineman hugged him tight.

"I'm so sorry, Jack, but you don't have a choice. Jillian is counting on you. Sieberling School is counting on you, too."

"But we don't have a chance!"

"How do you know that?"

Because Farnsworth said so himself. Unless . . .

"It doesn't matter," Jack sighed. "After tomorrow, I'm working toward something practical. Being the best pastry chef in the world was a stupid dream."

"No, it wasn't, Jack. It was *your* dream. We just didn't want you to get hurt. It's what parents do. And it's why we never told you about Farnsworth. Plus, we didn't think telling you would make any difference at the time. You were *so* obsessed about the Bonanza. We know you idolized him, but some people can be complicated. And sometimes it's important for you to find out things for yourself."

"Now I don't have a dream. Mom, what happens when someone you admire turns out to be a jerk?"

Jack's mother put her arm around his shoulder. "Then maybe it's time to find someone a little closer to your heart."

Jack reached into his pocket and pulled out the crumpled script he was supposed to read tomorrow.

He had an idea.

Chapter 27

Liz met the three teams in a waiting room outside the Samuel P. Ardmore Convention Center auditorium.

"Mr. Farnsworth wants to remind you to give it your best out there. This is not a taped and edited reality show. It's a live event. There are no retakes. What happens happens—for better or for worse."

Liz spoke directly to Jillian. "So choose your words carefully, because what you say will be on record forever."

As Jillian went out the door, Liz slipped a note into her hand. "From Mr. Farnsworth," she said.

In a restroom stall Jillian unfolded the paper and read: *Let's make this simple. Do as you've been asked and I will change your life forever. Refuse and you get <u>nothing</u>.*

Jillian shoved it into her apron pocket and joined Jack

on stage in the packed auditorium. Nothing could have prepared her for what she saw. Fifteen cameras were trained on the teams' three kitchen units. Three large video screens hung behind the judging table where Farnsworth stood with Liz and the trophies. Jillian turned to Jack. She had never seen her partner look so serious.

Two Sieberling students shoehorned into a ragged wild mustang costume galloped among the spectators. Chad buzzed around like a bee while leading a group of classmates in a chant he had written for the occasion:

> *At Sieberling, we sure can bake.*
> *There's nothing that our team can't make.*
> *But I wouldn't try Old Harbor's cake.*
> *Take one bite, your teeth will break!*

After the third time through the chant, Principal Dobkins rushed over and offered a stern warning. "From now on, all cheers will be limited to GO! SIEBERLING! GO! Violators will be asked to leave the auditorium and serve a week's detention." He also confiscated Chad's air horn and a bag of glitter.

The lights dimmed. A montage of images from past contests flashed on the video screens, followed by clips from the interviews with the contestants and their families.

Farnsworth stood behind the microphone and addressed the crowd. "Before our amazing young chefs begin, let me take this moment to thank all of you, the great people of Ardmore, for making this event such a success for the past seventy-four years. Take a good look at this stage. The future of our fair city is in capable hands."

The audience gave a rousing cheer.

Jack almost shouted the word his father used when he knew someone wasn't being truthful. It was a word he wasn't allowed to say, so he muttered the milder "bologna" under his breath.

"Without further ado, on with the competition! All of our bakers were asked to bring one item to help them today. Reginald, what's that interesting device you have there?"

"It's my Farnsworth Multi-Tier Cake Pan Junior," he said, reading off the teleprompter. "It's made from heavy-gauge steel and has a nonstick coating for easy cleanup when a budding baker like me gets messy in the kitchen."

"An excellent choice!"

Farnsworth turned to Veronica.

"And what did you bring to help you on your quest to become a baking champion?"

"I would be lost without my Farnsworth Perfect Pastry Brush Junior," Veronica said. "I adore its non-clumping silicone bristles, and my little hand fits perfectly around its contoured handle. It makes basting butter on biscuits or glazing donuts a dream."

"Another superb selection."

Quentin and Marcia of Feldspar also talked about items from Farnsworth's new line of gadgets—a citrus grater and a set of piping tips.

Then Farnsworth focused on Jack.

"And what did you bring?"

Jack pulled out a photograph from his apron pocket and held it up.

Farnsworth frowned as his face took on the hue of a radish.

"These are my great-grandparents Stan and Leah Goldfarb," Jack said, ignoring the teleprompter. Cameras zeroed in on the photo, which was projected on the screens above Farnsworth's glistening head. "Leah passed away before I was born, but I've been told she spent her days making pastries and breads in her shop— Goldfarb Bakery—at the corner of Market and Maple streets, right here in Ardmore. I'm sure you're familiar with the spot. People would travel miles to taste her cherry-covered cheesecakes and chocolate rugelach. She is my inspiration. Her entire life was about baking and bringing joy to others."

"How endearing." Farnsworth scowled.

To Jack, it looked like Farnsworth wanted to spring

from his chair and shred the photo into a million pieces.

"And what have you brought today to help you in the kitchen, Jillian?" Farnsworth asked. "Tell our audience the story behind it."

Jack glanced at Jillian's teleprompter. There were no words about blenders, sifters, or food processors. It was all about her mother and the pastry shop. The cameras closed in on her tearstained face. Trembling, she appeared to be on the verge of passing out.

Jillian held up the wooden spoon, which she had hidden in her sleeve. She looked at her father and started to speak.

"This spoon belonged to—"

"My great-grandmother Leah," Jack interrupted, looking directly at Farnsworth. "Since I could only bring one item, I gave Jillian the spoon. It's our good luck charm."

Farnsworth opened and closed his mouth several times as his eyes bored holes into the Sieberling School team. Finally he spat out, "Okay, let's move on . . ."

"Wait, I have something else I want to say," Jack continued, gazing into Jillian's eyes before turning back to Farnsworth. "Cooking is not a contest. It is a prayer whispered humbly as the sun rises."

"When no one else is looking," Jillian added. "When the rest of the world sleeps."

Farnsworth stormed off the stage as Liz took the microphone.

"Sit tight! We'll be right back with the start of the Bakerstown Bonanza!" she said.

"Thank you, Jack," Jillian said, looking relieved. "I would have done it for my dad, for you . . ."

"I know, but it wouldn't have been right."

"My mother would have liked you," Jillian said, taking Jack's hand in hers.

"Why?"

"Because you have a good heart."

Chapter 28

Trailed by Liz, Farnsworth returned to the stage. Jack could see it in his eyes: The results of the Bakerstown Bonanza were a done deal. Sieberling School was doomed to finish last—again. There would be no money, no fame, no immortality, and no recipe in the *Farnsworth Best of the Bonanza* cookbook.

I can live with that, Jack thought.

Farnsworth wore his phoniest grin as he addressed the competitors.

"I've been judging this contest for the last forty years. While we've had many amazing entries, I believe the young chefs of Ardmore can do even better. You will have three hours to create a dessert worthy of the Farnsworth name. I am expecting great things here today. Ladies and gentlemen, let the seventy-fifth Bonanza begin!"

The Old Harbor and Feldspar teams sprang into action.

Jillian stared down at her spoon, fingering the triangular notch missing from its top—*slightly broken, forever incomplete.*

Jack turned to Jillian and smiled.

"Let's make some chocolate rugelach," he said.

"Yes, for my mother and your great-grandmother."

"And for Ardmore, Ohio."

As Jillian combined the ingredients to make the dough, she heard her mother's voice whispering a suggestion.

"*You* add the flour, Jack," Jillian said. "Then stir with this." She held up the wooden spoon.

"Me? Are you sure?"

"Yes, I'm sure."

Jack closed his eyes and blended the ingredients, blocking out the whir of mixers, the clanging of pots, and the raised voices coming from the other teams' kitchens.

"Faster!" Veronica shouted at Reginald. "Why are you so slow today? This is for the big money. Remember, second place is *not* an option. We can't lose because of you. Hurry!"

Taking turns, Jack and Jillian worked the dough and then cut it into four sections before placing them in the refrigerator.

While the dough chilled, Jillian blended chocolate, cocoa, butter, sugar, salt, and cinnamon.

More shouts came from one of the other kitchens.

"350 degrees! Not 375! 350! Are you dense?" Marcia said.

"The recipe calls for 375," Quentin insisted. "And you're the one who put in too much butter!"

Jack rolled the dough into circles. Jillian coated them with the chocolate mixture. They each cut the dough into eight triangular-shaped pieces.

"These are not even at all," Jack said. "Farnsworth isn't going to like that."

"Don't worry. They're perfectly imperfect," Jillian said.

The sound of a baking pan crashing against a granite countertop echoed throughout the auditorium.

"No! No! No!" Veronica yelled, inspecting the baking pan for dents. "You're layering the icing too thick. It's an absolute disaster!"

"You're the absolute disaster!" Reginald shot back. "Do not question the artist!"

Jack and Jillian rolled their dough into crescent shapes, placed them on baking sheets, and put them in the oven.

"Now what?" Jack asked.

"Now we talk. Tell me about your great-grandmother."

Jack leaned up against the counter of their kitchen. He felt strangely calm, especially compared to the contestants from the rival schools. "My mother said her bubbe baked to survive. It was all she knew."

"She looks sad," Jillian said, examining the photograph.

"She was. This was the day they torn down Goldfarb Bakery. My mom is afraid I'll end up like her."

"You won't. Not if you love what you're doing. And not if you put love in what you bake."

"I was thinking of my great-grandmother baking in her kitchen as I was stirring," Jack said. "But I don't know if I did it right. Is that all there is to putting love in your cooking?"

"Not exactly. It's hard to explain. Like when Mom said, 'Cooking is not a contest,' I think she meant the reason behind *why* you bake is just as important as *how* you bake. Let's say you're making a batch of peanut butter cookies for a sick friend. It's the simplest recipe ever: one egg, a cup of white sugar, and a cup of peanut butter."

"I'd add a touch of sea salt, maybe extra-dark chocolate, and a smidge of chili powder. Now *that's* a peanut butter cookie," Jack said.

"You're missing the point. There's nothing special about the recipe. No fancy ingredients. No baking tricks required. But you still must want them to be the best peanut butter cookies ever made. By anyone. So you put your heart into it . . . when no one else is looking."

"Like your mother said."

"Yes. You make sure the ingredients are mixed just right. You test the batter for the ideal consistency. You ask questions: Are they soft and chewy but not too gooey? Are the edges crispy but not crumbly? And you always keep in mind who will be eating them. Not to impress anyone or win a trophy. But to—"

"Bring joy?" Jack said.

"Boom!" Jillian replied, giving him a high five. "Let's try this—together."

Jack and Jillian peeked in the oven and took in the full aroma of the chocolate rugelach. They watched the pastries turn golden brown as the chocolate bubbled between the layers of flaky dough. In an instant, Jillian was back in Joan of Hearts Pastry Shop, a time when her life seemed filled with endless possibilities. Jack imagined himself in Goldfarb Bakery, watching a young woman working in the kitchen, the sun rising outside her window. She smiled as she packaged boxes of rugelach for friends and family.

"It's time to finish up," Jillian said.

Jack pulled out the baking sheets and set each one on a cooling rack.

Jillian then arranged the cookies on a plain white tray. She laid her wooden spoon across the top and set the photograph next to it.

"Ten seconds left," Jack said.

He took Jillian's hand as they stared down at the simple chocolate-filled cookies—flawed, oddly shaped, and curious.

"One final touch," Jillian said.

She took a sifter, closed her eyes, and sprinkled a gentle dusting of powdered sugar on top.

Chapter 29

Jack and Jillian stared wide-eyed at the entries from Feldspar and Old Harbor. Quentin and Marcia had created a cake shaped like an electron microscope, complete with slides. Reginald and Veronica baked a four-tiered replica of the Farnsworth mansion. The letters *PF* were done in purple icing between the second and third layers of the cake. The top was a perfectly shaped dome covered in gold fondant. A red carpet made from strawberry glaze led up to two marzipan doors, which opened and closed on licorice hinges. The microscope and mansion cakes cast a long shadow over the plate of chocolate rugelach.

"Our young chefs have certainly approached this contest differently," Farnsworth said as he looked back and forth between the three desserts. "Which one do you think belongs on the cover of the *Farnsworth Best of the*

Bonanza cookbook? Marcia and Quentin, what is this spectacular creation you've made for us today?"

"It's our Cooking-Is-Chemistry Cake," Marcia said. "Other than the fact that it was baked at 375 degrees rather than 350 degrees, we followed the formula exactly."

"The temperature was ideal," Quentin said. "But don't be surprised if you taste two extra milligrams of butter in the frosting."

Farnsworth picked up one of the microscope's slides.

"This is most interesting," he said.

"Yes, that slide shows a common bacteria found in kitchens," Marcia said cheerfully. "It's invisible to the naked eye. Do you know how many bacteria are swimming on a kitchen sponge?"

"Millions!" Quentin said. "The slides are miniature sugar cookies. We used lemon and cream cheese icing for the bacteria. This one shows virus cells up close. It's made with real cherries because we go to a STEM school! Get it?"

Jack smiled. He knew that no matter how good the cake tasted, Farnsworth would never put a dessert featuring a multitude of microorganisms on the cover of his cookbook. As he took a bite, Farnsworth's expression didn't change at all.

Well, that leaves Sieberling School and Old Harbor Academy, Jack thought.

"Jillian and Jack, tell me about this fine plate of cookies you've prepared," Farnsworth said, tugging at his long goatee.

Jack recognized Farnsworth's sarcastic tone. "Fine" meant "pathetic," which meant, *You are losers.*

"It's chocolate rugelach, a traditional Jewish pastry," Jack said. "People started making it in Europe more than two hundred years ago. It was one of Leah Goldfarb's specialties. She delivered trays of it to families in Ardmore during Hanukkah."

"What a *sweet* story," Farnsworth said.

Jack knew that "sweet" meant "boring," which meant, *Poof, no viral videos or press coverage for you!*

"Jillian, *you* tell me why this chocolate rugelach should be on the cover of the *Farnsworth Best of the Bonanza.*"

He's giving me one last chance, Jillian thought. *Won't he ever admit defeat?*

"Because it is delicious," she said loudly and clearly.

"Many things are delicious. But why chocolate rugelach?"

"Because it will stay with you forever," she said, pausing to run her finger over the chipped spoon before gazing directly at the man scowling behind the microphone. "And, Mr. Farnsworth, this rugelach will help you to remember something very important that maybe you've forgotten."

For a brief second, a look of confusion flitted across

Farnsworth's face. "Well, this must be one powerful cookie." He winked as he held up a piece and took a small bite.

Farnsworth wanted to hate it. Despise it. After Jack and Jillian refused to read their prepared speeches, he had told Liz to get a close-up of his face as he bit into Sieberling School's "utter failure," whatever it was. He demanded that his look of disgust appear on all three video screens for the press and the town to watch in real time.

Even though Jack felt good about defying his former idol, the expression that formed on Farnsworth's face was one he never expected to see.

It was contentment. Peace. Innocence. Jillian saw it immediately. The chocolate and cream cheese had somehow flung open the top of Farnsworth's memory box, flooding him with his past—the smell in his kitchen when his nanny, Miss Alexandra, was making him chocolate brownies.

There was complete silence as Farnsworth savored the bite. The audience held their breath. Farnsworth brought the rest of the piece up to his face, staring at it as if he'd never seen a baked good like it. Then he popped it into his mouth and closed his eyes.

"Best try another one, just to make sure," he said, still chewing the first.

Same expression.

"There's a lot at stake here. We can't leave anything to

chance." So Farnsworth gobbled down a third piece and then a fourth.

A more bitter expression appeared on Farnsworth's face. It was a look that said, *There is no way this chocolate rugelach could have been baked by a pair of eleven-year-olds from Ardmore, Ohio. Not possible.*

"I hope you like them," Jillian said. "We've included a special ingredient."

"Well, I must say you've made a noble attempt," Farnsworth said, licking his fingers. "Bravo to both of you. Baking an exceptional rugelach can be tricky. Alas, it's a bit dry and not as light and flaky as I'd like it to be."

Jack knew that "dry" meant "the best rugelach I have ever eaten."

Farnsworth turned to Reginald and Veronica's four-tiered cake. He peeked around every corner and paused to admire the level of detail, right down to the cursive PF logo.

"For once, words escape me," Farnsworth said. "It's amazing what you can do with the right tools in the kitchen! Veronica, tell me about the cake."

"We wanted to make something as magnificent as the Farnsworth mansion. Everything we thought of seemed small and—"

"Pathetic?" Farnsworth said, glancing at the chocolate rugelach.

"Yes, small and pathetic in comparison. So we made a

cake of your family estate done in four layers, alternating between maple, banana, coconut, and vanilla fillings."

The top four flavors!!! I guess I'm not the only one who did the research, Jack thought.

"Not to use a cliché, but your cake looks almost too good to eat. But I must."

Farnsworth took a fork and plunged it into the top layer. It met little resistance as it speared the cake. A mixture of icing and undercooked batter ran off his fork and down his sleeve. He shoved the gooey clump as quickly as possible into his mouth.

"Mmmm, moist," he said. "Let's try another bite of this most delici—"

Before Farnsworth finished the word "delicious," the cake leaned to one side. The dome slid off and the rest of the layers oozed downward in slow motion. The PF morphed into a pool of crimson mush. With a loud *splat*, the mass fell onto the floor, covering Farnsworth's twenty-thousand-dollar shoes in red, purple, and gold.

The audience let out a collective gasp.

Farnsworth looked out into the crowd. All he saw were ten thousand flashing phones held aloft.

Wiping maple filling off his goatee, Farnsworth made a slashing motion with his hand and the video screens went blank. Then he charged off the stage.

"I'm announcing Reginald and Veronica as the winners!" Farnsworth yelled from the contestants' waiting room, the door closed so no one could hear him.

"But their cake was a disaster!" Liz said. "How about the Cooking-Is-Chemistry Cake?"

"Great idea, Liz. What's less appetizing than sugar cookie microscope slides showing viruses and bacteria? Nothing! That's what! So Old Harbor Academy's cake wins."

"But their cake *slid off the table*! It has never happened before!"

"I don't care. Jillian and Jack do not win. Period."

"But everyone saw it! Their families! The crew! And, by now, all social media sites!"

Farnsworth feverishly paced the floor. "Think! Think! Think! There has got to be a way out of this mess. There's *always* a way out."

Liz remained silent.

As Farnsworth rushed back onto the stage, he vowed, "I'm never coming back to Ardmore! Never!"

Farnsworth stood before Jack, Jillian, Veronica, Reginald, Marcia, and Quentin. In his hands he held three trophies, one for each winning baker and another twenty-inch trophy for the school.

The three teams' entries sat on the table beside him—

the half-eaten plate of chocolate rugelach, the microscope cake, and what was left of the mansion replica rescued from the floor and heaped back onto a tray.

Refusing to acknowledge Jack and Jillian, Farnsworth stared at Reginald and Veronica as he began.

"I can tell you from years of experience that being a successful businessman can be full of surprises. And surprises make life exciting. What we discovered here today is sometimes talented young people with big ideas and big dreams may reach too high, but their pursuit of greatness is what matters most. The Farnsworth food empire was built by taking chances and thinking outside the box. We learned from our failures. Where some see a disaster, I see a victory. Often our grandest mistakes are, in fact, our most glorious achievements. And those who reach for the stars ultimately rise to the top."

Reginald and Veronica smiled.

"With this in mind, I proudly present these trophies and the $150,000 check to . . ."

Farnsworth paused for dramatic effect, savoring the feeling of absolute power, his favorite part of the Bakerstown Bonanza—that moment before changing a life or crushing a dream with the utterance of a few words. He had done it for the last forty years, never once showing a hint of uncertainty. Once he had made up his mind, the final results were chiseled in stone.

But this time, before saying the names of the winning

team, the memory of that fantastic chocolate rugelach overwhelmed him. Farnsworth faltered.

"And the winners of the seventy-fifth anniversary of the Bakerstown Bonanza are Jillian Mermelstein and Jack Fineman of Sieberling School!" Farnsworth seemed shocked by his announcement, stunned by his own words. In a daze, he handed out the trophies and presented the oversize check to Jack and Jillian.

Balloons and confetti fell from the ceiling as Jack's parents hugged. Bruce jumped up and down as if he had won the PGA Championship. Grandma Rita and Mr. Mermelstein broke down in tears of joy. Farnsworth grabbed the plate of chocolate rugelach and retreated behind the stage. Students in Sieberling School's cheering section began a chant of "JACK AND JILLIAN! JACK AND JILLIAN! JACK AND JILLIAN!"

Everyone turned around as the sound of an earsplitting *HOOOOONNNNNNKKKKK!* filled the auditorium.

It was Principal Dobkins clutching Chad's air horn, a wide grin plastered to his face.

"Not for indoor use," Chad called out as blue and gold glitter rained down around them.

Liz appeared as the families gathered around Jack and Jillian.

"Congratulations to both of you!" she said. "There is one final step before you receive the $150,000. As mentioned in the contract, you will give us a copy of the winning recipe. Once Mr. Farnsworth makes it and is satisfied, the money is yours and the recipe will appear on the front cover of the cookbook."

Jillian wrote out the recipe and handed it to Liz.

"This is only a formality," Liz said. "We'll notify you when your check is ready."

ℭhapter 30

s Jillian got ready for school the next morning, Mr. Mermelstein received a call from Liz.

"We have a big problem. Mr. Farnsworth is furious. I've never seen him so upset—and I've seen it all. A limousine will arrive within the hour to take you to the convention center. He has been there all night! The Finemans are coming as well."

"What exactly is this big problem?" Mr. Mermelstein asked.

"There's no time to explain. Mr. Farnsworth will fill you in when you get here. Please hurry!"

When the Mermelsteins and Finemans arrived, they found Farnsworth hovering over one of the kitchen units. Plates of chocolate rugelach were scattered amongst mixing bowls, empty flour sacks, and measuring cups. Jillian's recipe lay in the middle of the chaos. Sweat clung to Farnsworth's scalp and splotches of batter stained his brow. His apron was streaked with chocolate smears.

"I have an issue with your chocolate rugelach recipe, Miss Mermelstein," Farnsworth said, barely controlling his anger.

"What's wrong?" Jillian asked. "Your batches look fine."

"That's where you're wrong," he said, his voice rising. "As you can see, I've made your chocolate rugelach a dozen times, followed your recipe exactly, but it doesn't taste anything like what you made."

"But you said ours was small and pathetic," Jillian said.

"Stop pretending," Farnsworth spat. "You and I both know your chocolate rugelach was extraordinary. That's why you won. But what's before you is not even ordinary."

Jillian sampled a piece. It tasted like gritty sand on a saltine cracker.

I was afraid this would happen, she thought.

Jillian scanned the recipe and saw the correct ingredients in the precise amounts.

"The recipe is fine the way it is."

"You're lying!" Farnsworth yelled. "You've left something out! What is it? If you don't tell me, you can say bye-bye to the money."

Grandma Rita tried to interrupt, but Farnsworth was on a roll.

He jabbed the air in Jillian's direction. "And as far as

making you the spokesperson for my 'Little Hands with Big Appetites' line, you can forget that, too! No commercials! No splashy ads in magazines! No trips around the world!"

"Spokesperson?" Jack said. "You never told me. And you're giving all that up? Why?"

Jillian shrugged. "It was never my dream."

Jack looked at Farnsworth. "It's not mine anymore, either."

Jillian's father had heard enough.

"You're a crook!" Mr. Mermelstein said. "The money belongs to Jack and Jillian. You can't take that away from them. We'll sue."

"Forget about suing him," Mr. Fineman said. "I'm going to sock him in the mouth."

"Stand aside. I get the first shot," Mrs. Fineman added, rolling up her sleeve.

"Did I mention that Grandma Rita also has a black belt in karate?" Jillian said.

"I wouldn't try it," Farnsworth said, wagging his finger. "You didn't read the contract carefully. If I can't duplicate the recipe, I have the right—*the discretion*—to deny the winners the money. My team of lawyers will back me up on this."

Discretion. That word again, Jillian thought.

"Go ahead, Jillian. Tell Farnsworth the secret ingredient," Jack urged.

"He'll never believe me."

"Oh, after today, I'll believe anything," Farnsworth said. "Come on, tell me the secret ingredient. What . . . did . . . you . . . leave . . . out?"

"It's not what *I* left out. It's what *you* left out—love."

"Did you say love?" Farnsworth snorted.

"Yes, love," Jack said. "Without it, your chocolate rugelach won't taste nearly as sweet. Nothing will. Jillian learned it from her mom and I learned it from Jillian."

Farnsworth's laughter filled the auditorium.

"That's preposterous! Absurd! The most ridiculous thing I've ever heard in all my years in the food industry!"

"But it's true!" Jillian said. "Why else are you having trouble making the chocolate rugelach?"

"Because it's missing a *real* ingredient, whatever that is. I'm calling my lawyers to disqualify both of you. Keep the trophies. They're made of cheap plastic, anyway. And no Culinary Education Center for your school, either. I have a flight to catch to Switzerland. So farewell to you all . . . and good riddance to Ardmore."

Jack and Jillian watched as Farnsworth turned and headed for the exit. They scanned the countertop where plates of the rugelach lay uneaten and inedible, searching for an answer amongst the jumble of Farnsworth's failed attempts.

Before he reached the door, Jillian shouted, "Mr. Farnsworth, please! We can help you make the chocolate rugelach the way you want it."

"I sincerely doubt that." Farnsworth laughed, not turning around. "And I told you, my time here is done. Now, goodbye!" He reached for the door handle.

"Say something else, Jillian! Anything!" Jack pleaded. "He's leaving!"

That's when the quiet girl who sat in the back row next to the storage closet reached deep within herself, filling the auditorium with the sound of an eleven-year-old who had come too far to simply give up.

"How would Miss Alexandra have made the chocolate rugelach?"

Farnsworth stopped. He slowly turned and faced Jillian and Jack.

"What . . . did . . . you . . . say?" His voice was hard, as if covered in ice.

This time Jillian spoke as gently as she could, recalling the sound of her mother's voice telling her that everything would work out.

"How would Miss Alexandra have made the chocolate rugelach?"

Farnsworth took a step backward, the mere mention of the name jabbing at his heart. He composed himself and staggered toward Jillian.

"I don't know what kind of game you're playing, young lady, but I don't like it. How could you possibly have known about Miss Alexandra?"

"You can learn a lot from a simple Google search,"

Jillian said. "Miss Alexandra used to tell you funny stories. Took you to the park. You went ice skating together. She baked you chocolate brownies—the best you'd ever eaten. You were her Little Cupcake. She loved you and you loved her. And nothing has ever been the same since she . . ."

Farnsworth's face burned red hot. He towered over Jillian, glaring downward.

"Those are *my* memories! Mine and only mine!" he wailed. "They belong to me! Not you, or Google, or anybody else. How dare you!"

Jillian stood tall and waited for the storm to pass.

"I'm sorry," she said. "I didn't mean to upset you." She reached up and grasped his hand. *Slightly broken. Forever incomplete.*

"I know exactly how you feel," she said.

Farnsworth slumped his shoulders, the weight of Jillian's words pressing down on him. Still holding Jillian's hand, he knelt to look her squarely in the eyes.

"I still miss her," he said. "I was only ten. None of it made any sense."

"Not everything in life is supposed to make sense," she replied.

"Could you show me how to use the special ingredient?" Farnsworth said, his anger subsiding. "I'm still not sure I believe it, but I'm willing to give it a last try."

"Jack and I will help," Jillian said. "Opening a memory box that's been closed for so long is hard. It's painful. That's why it's easier to keep it under lock and key. Do you think you can remember?"

"Memory box?"

"We'll explain. Are you ready?"

"Yes, I'm ready."

"Alright then. Let's bake something—together."

Everyone watched Phineas Farnsworth III, flanked on either side by Jack and Jillian, take his place behind the counter where he had spent the night trying to replicate the chocolate rugelach.

"There's nothing unusual about these ingredients," Jillian said. "They're the same ones you used in your last twelve attempts."

"So what do I do differently?" Farnsworth asked, tying on a fresh apron.

"Before you bake, think about *why* you're making the rugelach," Jillian said. "Then put your heart into every step."

Farnsworth blended the cream cheese and butter to make the dough before mixing in sugar, salt, vanilla extract, and flour.

"Now close your eyes and think of your best memory with Miss Alexandra," Jack said.

"That's easy. It was when . . ."

"Don't tell us," Jillian said. "That's private. You can pull it out of your memory box whenever you need it. File it under A—for Alexandra."

With each step of the recipe, Farnsworth found a new memory to add. Sometimes he chuckled as he stirred. Other times he wiped away tears. Near the end he doubled over in laughter.

Farnsworth let Jack and Jillian pull the rugelach out of the oven.

"You're the experts, after all," Farnsworth said.

"These smell wonderful," Jillian said.

"Yes," Jack agreed. "But how do they taste?"

Once the rugelach cooled, Farnsworth arranged them on a large platter.

"Go ahead," Jack said. "Try one."

"Actually, I didn't make this batch for myself," Farnsworth said, carrying the tray over to Grandma Rita for the initial taste. "They're my gift to all of you."

One by one, everyone had a piece . . . or two . . . or three. The reviews were unanimous.

"Mmmm . . . this is . . ." Grandma Rita searched for the right word.

"Indescribable?" Mr. Mermelstein asked.

"Yes," she said. "In fact, indescribably amazing!"

The tray eventually made its way back to Jack, Jillian, and Farnsworth.

"You go first," Farnsworth urged.

Jack and Jillian took small nibbles and scrunched up their faces.

"Alas, it's a bit dry," Jillian said, imitating Farnsworth.

"Not as light and flaky as I'd like, but a noble effort nonetheless," Jack followed. "Making rugelach can be tricky, you know."

Farnsworth's face drooped until he saw Jack and Jillian struggling to hold back giggles.

"You got me. I guess I deserved that," Farnsworth said.

Then he ate the last piece on the tray—a lopsided crescent, the outcast of the batch—like the lonely student in the back of the class who's ready to move to the front row.

"It's as fine as the rugelach you made," Farnsworth said, licking chocolate from his fingers. "As wonderful as Miss Alexandra's chocolate brownies. The prize money is yours."

Everyone let out a cheer.

"And each school will receive a Culinary Education Center," he continued. "It's only fair."

"And the recipe?" Jack asked.

"It will go in the cookbook as written," Farnsworth said.

"Not quite," Jillian said.

She took the recipe from the counter. Across the top she wrote, *Joan Mermelstein's Extraordinary Chocolate Rugelach*. Then she added one final ingredient: *Sprinkle in lots of love—at your own discretion.*

❧Chapter 31

Six months later, Jack and Jillian, now seventh-graders, were the guests of honor at the ribbon-cutting ceremony for Sieberling School's new Culinary Education Center. Because Jack's videos had gone viral, Zombie Brunch's only album had been rereleased. The band, older and grayer than when the album originally came out, played on the school's front lawn as people arrived. Soon, everyone was answering each other's questions with, "Yeah, yeah, yeah, yeah, yeah, yeah, yeah."

For the celebration, parents, teachers, and students brought baked goods set up on tables near the entrance.

Grandma Rita arrived carrying a blueberry pie.

"Don't worry," Jillian told Jack. "We can now add pie making to Grandma's list of skills. I barely helped."

"At least no emergency vehicles showed up," said Mr. Mermelstein, setting down a plate of Chewy Raspberry

Almond Cookies. "I know it's not the beginning of the week, but these are good anytime."

Bruce, who wore a new pair of silver-and-sky-blue pants for the occasion, had finally come to the conclusion that baking wasn't a waste of time after all. He held a tin of oatmeal cookies he baked that morning.

"These don't have anything *unusual* in them?" Principal Dobkins asked.

Bruce smiled, revealing nothing but specks of raisins sticking to his teeth. "No, they're cricket-free, but I think I actually miss the crunch."

Mr. and Mrs. Fineman brought a cherry-covered cheesecake.

"From my Bubbe Leah's recipe. I added the extra love, too," Mrs. Fineman said.

Liz brought a rhubarb pie made from the recipe of the first Bonanza winner, Edna Harberg, back in 1944.

"I wore her apron as I baked. I borrowed it from the Farnsworth mansion. It still has the stain right near the pocket."

Jack guided a forkful of pie into his mouth.

"Blissfully divine," he said.

Chad made a key lime pie with a graham cracker crust. Ms. Riedel ate two pieces.

"I did zees from scratch," he said, doing another poor imitation of Francois Furveau. "Mz. Riedel, you will have three minutes to duplicate zees recipe . . . now *go!*"

Jack and Jillian baked the Mixed-Up Scrabble Babble Cake.

"This was too good not to make again," Jack said. "And we did it together."

In the weeks after the contest, Jack and Jillian continued their baking sessions, experimenting with new recipes and perfecting those in Jillian's tattered recipe book. They talked about using some of the prize money to someday open a little pastry shop near the spot of Goldfarb Bakery.

"I've got it! We'll call it the Chirping Cricket!" Jack said.

"The chirping *what*?"

"The Chirping Cricket. The name of our pastry shop."

"I like it," Jillian said. "But first we have to make it out of seventh grade. Important math test tomorrow, remember?"

"Gotta dream big. Gotta dream big."

After the ceremony, Liz approached Jack and Jillian holding a plate of chocolate rugelach and two wrapped gifts.

"Mr. Farnsworth made this special for you," she said. "He would have come today, but he didn't want to take the spotlight away from you both."

Jack opened the wrapping paper on the box marked *For Jack* and pulled out a copy of the rare 1983 *Farnsworth Best of the Bonanza* cookbook, the one with the typo that was never released to the public.

He turned to the inside front cover, where there was a short note on top of the page.

"That's Farnsworth's handwriting," Jillian said. "I'd recognize it anywhere."

Jack read out loud:

Dear Jack,

I recall from your application how much you wanted this book. I believe it is the only one in existence. I had all the others destroyed to erase the mistake. But as I've discovered, some mistakes can't be eliminated—and I've certainly made my share of them, much bigger than a simple misspelling. Keep this book as my gift to you. May it help you learn from a man who has erred in so many ways, both large and small.

Phineas Farnsworth III

Inside the second box with Jillian's name on it, she found an advance copy of the seventy-fifth edition of the *Farnsworth Best of the Bonanza* cookbook. As promised, a photo of Jillian's mother's chocolate rugelach filled the front cover. A note attached read:

Dear Jillian,

I do not expect you, or anyone else, to ever forgive me for my cruel behavior. An apology at this point is futile. Instead, I will say thank you and provide a brief explanation of why I am who I am. When Miss Alexandra, my beloved nanny, passed away, I was only ten years old. While my parents

223

tended to the family business, she looked after me, baked for me, sang to me, and filled my heart with a gladness I have not felt again until only recently. Your chocolate rugelach brought her back to me—made me feel alive again. And for this I will be eternally grateful.

Phineas Farnsworth III

Jack popped a piece of the chocolate rugelach into his mouth.

"Extraordinary," he said.

"Yes, extraordinary," Jillian agreed.

Joan Mermelstein's Extraordinary Chocolate Rugelach

Makes 32 Rugelach

Prep: Preheat oven at 350°. Place parchment paper on cookie sheet.

Pastry Ingredients:
- 8 oz. cream cheese, at room temperature
- ½ lb. unsalted butter (2 sticks), at room temperature
- ¼ cup granulated sugar
- ¼ teaspoon salt
- 1 teaspoon vanilla extract
- 2 cups all-purpose flour

Cream the cream cheese and butter in a bowl until light and smooth. Add sugar, salt, and vanilla extract. Add flour and mix until just combined. Roll into a ball and cut into quarters. Wrap each quarter section in plastic and refrigerate for one hour.

Filling Ingredients:
- 6 oz. semisweet chocolate bar
- 2 tablespoons butter
- 2 tablespoons unsweetened cocoa
- 5 tablespoons granulated sugar
- 1 tablespoon cinnamon
- Pinch of salt

Break up chocolate bar into small pieces and place in top of a double boiler on low to medium heat. Add butter and stir until melted. Take off heat and add remaining ingredients. Stir until smooth.

On a well-floured board, use a rolling pin to roll one portion of dough into a nine-inch circle. Spread the chocolate filling evenly over the surface, leaving 1/8 inch of uncovered dough around the edge. Cut circle into eight wedges. Starting at the wide end, roll each wedge and place on the cookie sheet, with the point end tucked under. Repeat for the remaining portions of dough.

Egg Wash Ingredients:
- 1 egg
- 1 tablespoon milk

Whisk egg and milk. Using a pastry brush, brush egg wash on each rugelach.

Bake for 15 to 20 minutes or until golden brown. Cool cookies on wire rack for 10 minutes. Sprinkle with powdered sugar—and lots of love, at your own discretion.

Fineman's Fine Butterscotch Basil Brownies

Makes about 16 Brownies

Prep: Preheat oven at 350°.

Brownie Ingredients:
   1 cup brown sugar, firmly packed
   ¾ cup flour
   ¼ cup butter
   1 egg
   1 teaspoon baking powder
   ½ teaspoon salt
   ¾ cup butterscotch chips
   1 heaping tablespoon fresh chopped basil
   1 teaspoon vanilla extract

Melt butter and brown sugar on low heat, stirring until sugar is dissolved. Cool to room temperature. Add egg. Place flour, salt, baking powder, and chopped basil in a small bowl and whisk carefully. Add dry ingredients to butter and brown sugar. Stir in butterscotch chips. Add vanilla extract and stir. Spread evenly in a square eight-inch greased pan. Bake at 350° for 25 minutes. Cool for 10 minutes before spreading frosting.

Frosting Ingredients:
    2 cups powdered sugar
    1 stick butter, softened
    2 teaspoons vanilla extract
    1 tablespoon milk
    ½ teaspoon cinnamon

Beat sugar and butter until smooth. Blend in vanilla and milk until spreadable. Stir in cinnamon. Spread evenly on brownies and enjoy!

Oooh La La Lemon Bars

Makes about 24 bars

Prep: Preheat oven at 350°.

Crust Ingredients:
    2 cups flour
    ½ cup confectioner's sugar
    1 cup butter
    ¼ teaspoon vanilla extract

Crust: Mix flour, confectioner's sugar, butter, and vanilla extract with a pastry blender. Pat "crumbly" batter into 9 inch x 12 inch greased pan and bake at 350° degrees for 20 minutes. Let cool for 10 minutes.

Filling Ingredients:
  4 eggs
  2 cups sugar
  ¼ cup flour
  1 teaspoon baking powder
  ⅓ cup fresh lemon juice

Filling: Blend eggs, sugar, and lemon juice. Beat until thick. Add flour and baking powder. Pour over finished crust and bake for 25 minutes at 350°. When cool, sprinkle with powdered sugar. Cut into squares with wet knife.

Acknowledgments

The $150,000 Rugelach began as an inside family joke. What if we created a Jewish grandmother who was so baking-impaired that her attempts at making a simple blueberry pie brought emergency vehicles rushing to her door? Good start, we thought. Better yet, let's give her a granddaughter with extraordinary skills in the kitchen and see how the plot, uh, cooks. It was quickly decided that our kindhearted comic foil would be named Grandma Rita.

Now here's the punchline: The real Grandma Rita, Wayne's mother, is a baker of supreme gifts—a wizard with a whisk, a maven with a mixer. So much love radiates from her Hanukkah dessert tables that to gaze upon one is to stare directly into a thousand suns. Hyperbolic? Try a thick slice of her lemon roll or a piece of her cherry-covered cheesecake and then we'll talk.

Beyond inspiring us with her baked goods, Rita Marks has been a thoughtful reader, patient listener, and, like her fictional namesake, the most loving grandma, mother-in-law, and mother anyone could ever hope for.

We are also forever indebted to all those who have provided us with heaping tablespoons of support: our children, Claire and Elliott; Allison's father, Chet Geary; our siblings Craig Marks, Pat Johnson, and David Geary; Ellen and Abby Marks, who have shared many a laugh with us at holiday gatherings; book critique friends Meryl Gordon and Tami Lehman-Wilzig; and dear friends and generous readers Lois Reaven and Lisa Bansen-Harp.

Special shout-outs go to Catriella Freedman, Rachel Goodman, and everyone at PJ Our Way for believing in our work and helping to put our stories in the hands of young readers. We have a double batch of gratitude for the team at Yellow Jacket, especially Brett Duquette and Courtney Fahy, who encouraged us to take the story to places never imagined. And a million thanks to Ariel Landy, whose illustrations spectacularly bring *The $150,000 Rugelach* to life.

Lastly, it is our deepest regret that Wayne's father, Burton Marks, could not be here to see the book in print. A sweet, humble man and author of his own children's books (co-written with his wife, Rita), he reveled in our talks about how to handle plotting and pacing. Even in his last days, his eyes would light up when our discussions turned to the struggles and joys of writing. He is greatly missed by all.

Allison and Wayne Marks

11/22